DEATH ON THE BOZEMAN

One year after the end of the Civil War, three southerners are heading northwest on the Bozeman Trail to the gold mining camp at Virginia City. When they find the army has closed the trail because the Sioux are on the warpath, they accept work at Fort Phil Kearny. After an Indian ambush, the men flee the fort, together with a man called Slade. But when Slade is revealed as a hired gun and murderer, the southerners are drawn into the hunt to apprehend him to clear their names.

PAUL BEDFORD

DEATH ON THE BOZEMAN

Complete and Unabridged

LINFORD
Leicester

First published in Great Britain in 2017 by
Robert Hale
an imprint of The Crowood Press
Wiltshire

First Linford Edition
published 2020
by arrangement with
The Crowood Press
Wiltshire

A catalogue record for this book is available
from the British Library.

ISBN 978–1–4448–4493–1

Published by
Ulverscroft Limited
Anstey, Leicestershire

Set by Words & Graphics Ltd.
Anstey, Leicestershire
Printed and bound in Great Britain by
T. J. International Ltd., Padstow, Cornwall

This book is printed on acid-free paper

For my good friend Eric Sykes.
Many thanks for all your help and
advice along the way!

1

Maybe it was just the natural feel-good factor of a summer's day, but the Territory of Wyoming sure seemed like a beautiful place to be. The lush grassland and tall pine trees of the Powder River country spread around them for as far as the eye could see, and there was a freshness to the land that made a man feel good inside. Maybe the folks in the north had had something tangible to fight for after all. Then again, *their* continued liberty had never been in doubt.

'Are you even listening to me?' complained Charlie Pickett with a good show of mock severity. Such a display would have been impossible before the war, when his youthful good looks had seemed to be permanently crinkled with a grin.

Waylan Summers just laughed and continued to soak up the warm sun. He knew that he'd been daydreaming, but

1

how could that be a crime on such a glorious day? It was left to the ever-serious Taylor Johnston to answer.

'He's off with the fairies as usual,' that man remarked, his pockmarked brow deeply furrowed. 'I'll wager he's already forgotten everything that Yankee lieutenant warned us about.'

Waylan lazily fixed his startling blue eyes on his friend and asked with studied innocence, 'You mean how we should watch out for Red Cloud's savage hordes, because we ain't never seen anything like them? Oh, I can recall every word. I just don't reckon we're going to get our scalps lifted today, that's all. It's just too damned pretty out here!'

'It sure *was*,' chipped in Charlie ominously, as he suddenly peered intently up the greatly travelled trail a-ways. The well-worn saddle leather creaked as he rose up in the stirrups for a better view. 'Only now we're about to get some visitors, and eighteen months ago I'd have popped a cap on them for sure.'

The day's pleasures were abruptly

forgotten as all three men scrutinized the unwelcome newcomers. There were eleven riders in total, and all wore Union blue. A grizzled sergeant was in the lead, followed by ten other enlisted men in a column of twos formation. Most of them held Springfield Rifles canted awkwardly across their saddle horns and were uneasily scrutinizing their surroundings, rather than the three white men ahead. That in itself told the watching southerners two things: the soldiers were mounted infantry rather than cavalry, and there was trouble brewing. The question was . . . for whom?

'Those sons of bitches look kind of twitchy to me,' remarked Taylor. He was only half joking when he added, 'What say we drop a few of them and get the hell out of here?'

'That dreadful war is over, so let's leave it that way,' replied Waylan firmly. His good humour had evaporated at the sight of the hated blue uniforms. 'We're businessmen now, or at least we will be. The last thing we need is a fight with the God-damned Yankee army.'

Keeping their hands well clear of any firearms, the three men gently reined in their horses and with studied calm waited for the soldiers to fetch up before them.

* ★ ★

As he closely observed the three civilians, Sergeant Rudabauer's features wore a 'seen it all' look that most veterans affected in front of their men. He noted the lean physiques, the way they held themselves, and more particularly their weapons. The old soldier had a pretty damn good idea of both who they were and what they had been, but asked the question anyway: 'Just what brings you fellas out along the Bozeman on this fine day?'

Charlie just couldn't help himself. 'What's it to you blue bellies? Since the Surrender we've gone where we please. In fact we did pretty much that *before* the Surrender!'

Taylor scowled his agreement and

ostentatiously stroked the stock of his Henry repeating rifle.

Rudabauer nodded slowly, as though agreeing with himself. 'I knew it. Johnny Rebs. Even without your butternut forage caps, I could spot you a mile off.' He paused for a moment, choosing his next words carefully. 'Well, I reckon I'll tell you boys something you might just thank me for, because since that Surrender we're all supposed to be on the same side. Citizens of these United States, you might say. You've done wandered into an all-out Indian war, and Colonel Henry B. Carrington, God bless his socks, has seen fit to close this road to civilian traffic until further notice. For your own safety as much as his convenience. How's that sound to you?'

Charlie never got the chance to respond to that, because it suddenly became very apparent just who the real leader of the three southerners was. Waylan made a sharp cutting motion with his hand and momentarily glared at his two companions. Yet his reply, when it came, was far

5

more measured and restrained.

'Don't you pay my friends any heed, Sergeant. They've just got some bad feelings coming up from the recent conflict. It must have been the sight of your uniforms. Isn't that right, fellas?'

His two companions grunted sourly, but held their peace. Swiftly he moved on. 'We're heading northwest for Virginia City and we were told that the Bozeman Trail is the easiest route. Thought we'd try our luck prospecting in Alder Gulch. Hear tell there's gold nuggets just waiting to be picked up off the ground, for those plucky enough to make the journey.'

In spite of the obvious tension, the 'non-com' couldn't restrain a chuckle. 'Yeah, well, we've lost a few woodcutters to gold fever lately . . . amongst other things, but you really can't believe all that you hear in this life. And I suppose those that told you it was easiest, carried on westward on the Oregon Trail, well away from this pretty little snake pit.'

Waylan matched the sergeant's apparent change of mood by smiling broadly. 'I know that every gold or silver strike is exaggerated, but we don't know any other trade than soldiering. We've got to do something to earn a crust, short of turning outlaw, and the journey don't scare us none.'

The soldier returned his smile, but what that man said next had the uncomfortable hint of a command about it. 'So come and work for the US Army for a while. There's plenty of galvanized Yankees doing just that in these parts. After all, a man's got to eat, huh?'

Waylan sensed the intake of breath from his companions, but managed to maintain a friendly demeanour. 'Thanks, Sergeant, but we'll pass. We've got business elsewhere and we can look after ourselves.'

The other man's smile abruptly slipped and his expression became bleak. 'I guess you just didn't hear me when I said the colonel had closed the road. He's got a fight on his hands for sure and doesn't need a load of civilians stumbling around. So you *Confederate* sons of bitches have really only got two choices. You can either turn around and go back home, wherever that is, or sign on for a spell of woodcutting. That'll get you three squares a day and some gov'ment script.'

Waylan's features turned to ice. 'There is actually a third choice,' he remarked with quiet menace. 'Since we've no home left to go to, we could use these fancy repeaters to blow you all to hell!'

At a nod from their sergeant, the ten troopers behind him slowly formed a semi-circle, their single shot rifles suddenly aimed threateningly at the three southerners. And yet Rudabauer made no move for the revolver in his covered holster. Instead he shook his head sadly. 'Yeah, I guess you could at that. But is that really what you want? Odds on you won't all survive, and whoever does will be on the dodge for the rest of their miserable lives . . . for one good reason. *We ain't at war any more!*'

Waylan regarded him steadily as he

absorbed the sound and apparently genuine advice. Yet it wasn't the well-reasoned words that caused him to frown. Deep in the trees, a bird whistled shrilly. There was something derisive in the sound that caused him far more discomfort than any number of Union soldiers, because he had used enough bird calls in his time to know which were human and which not. And he wasn't the only one who'd heard it. He glanced at his startled companions and then back to the non-com. What he saw caused his eyes to widen like saucers. The sergeant's grizzled face registered stark fear that had nothing to do with confronting former enemies.

'If you three fellas know what's good for you,' Rudabauer snapped, 'You'll hightail it back to the fort with us, pronto. You might think you've been in some real tough fights before, but you ain't ever seen the like of those murdering devils. They strike like chain lightning and butcher a man worse than any Minie ball could.' With that, he motioned to his men and turned away, the three southerners apparently no longer of any interest. As the column moved off, he called back, 'Consider yourselves warned!'

As the army detail rapidly retraced its steps, Waylan and his friends carefully scanned the tree line. He was very conscious of the fact that none of them had actually seen the supposed threat, but then they hadn't survived a bloody Civil War by ignoring their intuition.

'That sergeant didn't look like someone who'd spook easily,' Waylan remarked. 'I guess it wouldn't do any harm to check out this fort of theirs, until we know what we're up against. If it don't suit, we can always move on.'

'You reckon?' Taylor queried, his eyes like gimlets.

'I reckon!'

2

The three men had a lot to take in, but it was the awesome boom of a mountain howitzer that abruptly claimed all their attention. Instinctively twisting in their saddles to catch the fall of shot, they watched the shell burst some few hundred yards down their back trail. However, it wasn't the unexpected sound of a big gun that brought a chill to their spines — they had encountered plenty of those in years past. Rather it was the sight of a large band of half-naked horsemen, as they rapidly wheeled about and dashed for cover in the trees. Their presence confirmed that the soldiers had been fully justified in fleeing the dubious birdcall.

Just to one side of the smoking field piece stood an officer wearing the uniform of a full colonel. His bearded features were creased with anxiety as he observed the retreating Indians.

'Re-load and stand ready,' he called over to a waiting lieutenant. Another officer muttered something and Carrington, for it could only have been he, snapped back, 'There will be *no* pursuit. Those devils are likely seeking to draw us out over the ridge and into an ambush!'

From the pained expressions on his subordinates' faces, his words were not well received, but the new arrivals were given no opportunity to consider the implications of that.

'The 'gun that shoots twice' is about the only thing we've got that scares those God-damn sons of bitches,' declared Sergeant Rudabauer. Having reached relative safety, he had left his enlisted men to their own devices and joined the southerners. 'Welcome to Fort Phil Kearny,' he continued. 'It ain't much to look at yet, but at least there's safety in numbers . . . I guess.'

In truth, with only twenty-odd yards of stockade erected, 'Fort' Phil Kearny was little more than an encampment.

Rows of tents had been pitched in the luxuriant grassland between the forks of the Little Piney and Big Piney creeks. There was ample timber available, but therein lay the rub: the fort had to be constructed near an adequate source of drinking water, on open ground, with a good field of fire and well away from the tree line, which meant that the logging crews had to travel beyond the protection of their artillery.

As veterans of the Petersburg defences, the three ex-soldiers recognized the ramifications immediately and began to realize why additional labourers might be welcome. As it was, with the Indians again out of sight, the incessant sawing and hammering resumed, as work on the fortifications continued.

'How come I ain't seen any cavalry?' Taylor queried. 'Seems to me you couldn't do without them in country like this.'

Rudabauer grunted. 'Huh. You'd think so, wouldn't you? Only thing is, the officers say that we haven't come out here to fight. The 18th Infantry is tasked with building and manning three forts. That's why it's commanded by an engineer, with little experience of battlefield command. So all we've got is a few units of the 2nd Cavalry and they're spread very thin, what with keeping open communications an' all.'

Before the others could comment, the sergeant spotted an approaching officer and stiffened slightly. 'This here's Captain Brown, the quartermaster. You keep your secessionist mouths shut and leave the talking to me.'

The officer who strode up to join them had fair receding hair and, like his commanding officer, a full beard. He glanced briefly at the new arrivals. 'Who are these men, sergeant?'

Rudabauer snapped off a salute. 'Prospectors caught up in the conflict, sir. They've agreed to work on the logging details until the colonel gives them safe passage.'

Brown scrutinized the men more closely. 'Prospectors, huh. Well, there's no gold around here, just hostiles. So you might find a use for those fancy repeaters.'

Waylan smiled thinly, but kept his eyes averted and his mouth shut as instructed. He had little desire for his southern accent to invite hostility. Sadly, Charlie Pickett just couldn't keep his own tongue bridled.

'We ain't exactly *willing* volunteers, blue belly,' he growled.

Brown's expression noticeably hardened as he absorbed such blatant disrespect. He favoured Charlie with an icy smile. 'Ah, I see. So that's how it is. Well you *gentlemen* can head back to the Platte anytime you God damn please, *without* an army escort. But while you're on the Bozeman, you are under army jurisdiction and you'll follow orders or suffer the consequences.' Switching his attention back to Rudabauer, he continued, 'Sergeant, assign them to Hoffman's detail. The corporal will know how to make them welcome.' With that, he turned on his heels and stalked off towards the headquarters tent.

Rudabauer shook his head. 'You need to learn when to curb your tongue, young fella. Follow me, all of you.'

Peering out from under a battered slouch hat, one of the civilian workers had witnessed the minor altercation with more than casual interest. His name was Slade, which was about as much information as most people ever got out of him. He, too, had designs on the Alder Gulch gold strike, but not in the way that most decent folks would. And because of that, he therefore had more than just the obvious reason not to be travelling alone through an Indian uprising. Since it appeared that the three newcomers had the same destination in mind, as well as having no love for Yankee soldiers, it made plenty of sense to team up. At least until he found out what kind of men they were.

As Rudabauer and the southerners came closer, Slade ceased honing his axe and called out, 'You can leave these boys with me, sergeant. I'll right gladly show them the ropes.'

The non-com peered at him suspiciously before growling, 'You get that *blade* any sharper *Slade* and you'll be able to slice beef with it.' He turned away, overly pleased with his sparkling wit, but then called back over his shoulder, 'Don't go looking for trouble, fellas. There's more than enough to go around out here!'

For a few moments no one said anything. They were too occupied assessing each other. Waylan for one decided that it was a long time since he'd seen a tougher-looking hombre. This Slade was a bull of a man, with massive shoulders and trousers straining against equally impressive thighs. Probably aged around thirty, he had the look of a man completely at home in the wilderness and therefore very likely dangerous to cross . . . just like the terrain.

Slade in turn saw three young men aged beyond their years by their experiences. All carried Henry rifles and he had no doubt that they were proficient in their use, which had to be a good thing in Indian country. The question was, did they enjoy using them? Searching for the likely leader, his glance settled on Waylan Summers' tall figure. There was something about his posture that made him stand out from his companions, and when Slade locked on to the other man's piercing blue eyes he knew that he was correct.

'Now that we've all had a good look-see,' the huge man remarked, 'How's about we all share some names?' So saying, he stood up to shake hands, and his grip was bone crushing.

Only Waylan briefly managed to match the pressure, whereas his companions were left counting their fingers. With the 'howdy dos' out of the way, he came directly to the point. 'I don't figure you for a nursemaid, mister, and we ain't neighbours that I know of, so what's your angle?'

Slade favoured him with a knowing smile. 'That's what I like. A man who cuts straight to the chase. Well, I'll tell you. The way I see it, these soldier boys are gonna get their asses kicked. Carrington doesn't seem to realize it, but this post is under siege and us civilians don't even figure in his thinking. If we're all going to survive to pan any gold, we need to stick together. Savvy?'

Waylan grunted his understanding. 'Seems like you don't miss much, mister. So when do they put us to work? And what's this Hoffman like?'

'Well, after chasing that bunch off of Lodge Trail Ridge, I don't reckon they'll risk a logging detail today. We'll likely be sent out at first light. As for Hoffman, he's some sort of Prussian son of a bitch trying to make a name for himself. Reckons to have been an officer back in the day, but if you ask me he's hiding something . . . like ability.'

At that very moment, an unusually well turned out non-com with two sky-blue chevrons on each arm strode officiously up to them. Despite the warmth, the top button of his jacket was fastened, forcing more colour into his florid cheeks.

'The sergeant haf told me you are the new men vor my detail,' he barked out with a noticeably guttural delivery. 'You vill be ready at break of day, ya? Do not think that because you are civilians you can provoke me. And bring those rifles. You might need them!' Then, without having even asked their names, the corporal departed, his back ramrod straight.

As the four reluctant recruits watched him go, a smile spread across Taylor's face. He was often times chided over his serious demeanour, but even he could see the funny side of the very brief encounter. Displaying a talent that his friends hadn't suspected, he suddenly remarked, 'You vorthless scum. Ve haf vays of making you vork!'

His audience of three burst into raucous laughter, but then as it died away they all settled into contemplative silence. The coming day could well see them having to do far more than just fell trees.

As the new day dawned, fourteen wagons pulled out of the environs of Fort Phil Kearny. With barely a cloud in the sky, it was shaping up to be a hot one, and quite possibly in more than one sense of the word. Riding on the heavy wagons were twenty-one soldiers and nine civilians. In addition to ropes, pulleys, axes and two-man saws, they all carried rifles. Colonel Carrington, seemingly habitually drawn and anxious, watched them depart. None of the men were in any doubt about what could be waiting for them, and as they rattled off towards the distant trees many of them glanced back longingly at the busy encampment.

Keeping his voice low, Slade remarked, 'If all hell breaks loose, whatever else these silly bastards do, use the wagons as cover. Don't try saving the animals. They belong to the army, not us. And let's try and stick together, huh?'

Waylan nodded, but made no comment, for in truth he had not yet made his mind up about the big man. The previous evening the four of them had companionably shared a campfire. Slade had cheerfully regaled them with tales of his past exploits, but strangely the four-year long Civil War hadn't figured in them at all. It could have been because he was avoiding a touchy subject with three southerners, but somehow Waylan didn't think so. Still, for better or worse, they were all in it together, and the southerner liked to be prepared.

Glancing at Slade's old Spencer, he observed, 'I ain't never fought Indians before, but I reckon if it comes to a fight, these repeaters of ours need to fill the gaps when those muzzle-loaders are being reloaded. Otherwise we'll get over-run for sure.'

The big man favoured him with an ambiguous smile. 'I'm kind of new to all this myself,' he replied, not altogether convincingly. 'I'll follow your lead and with luck we'll all be back hunkering around that campfire tonight, just like good friends should.'

It wasn't lost on any of the three southerners that their new acquaintance was, without even a 'by your leave', now promoting himself as a good friend. Where they came from, men had to earn that right.

*   *   *

'Is that a leaning axe or a using axe? 'Cause if you move any slower, you'll be doing yesterday's work.'

Waylan involuntarily jumped with surprise, before turning to look at the blue-clad figure. The private who had spoken so eloquently wore a cheery smile, and with good reason. Unlike most of his comrades he was on guard duty and therefore not drenched in sweat, as were the others.

'It don't concern me none,' the soldier continued amiably. 'Just don't let Hoffman catch you slacking, is all. Otherwise he'll forget that you're not in uniform and have you tied to a wagon wheel.'

Waylan grinned and nodded his thanks. As his friends could confirm, it wasn't the first time he'd been caught day-dreaming since arriving in the glorious Powder River country.

'I can see why the Sioux would want to fight for all this,' he remarked. 'If it was mine, I know I would.'

Having been brought back to reality, the reluctant labourer glanced around the clearing. Already a number of trees had been felled and were being stripped of their foliage ready for transportation back to the garrison. Ideally, such a day should have been spent lazing next to one of the many rivers in the region, but it was not to be. He had to admit that Hoffman appeared to know his business, at least superficially. The wagons had been wheeled around on open grassland to form a rough defensive circle and also act as a corral for the animals. Admittedly they had dense woodland on three sides, but then there could be no avoiding that. It was, after all, the fort's voracious need for timber that had brought them there. Each man had his rifle close by and sentries had been posted; not that they could really see a lot.

As Waylan hefted his axe, one of the sweating enlisted men called out to the guard, 'Hey, Jud. Don't you think Nelson's been in those trees a powerful long time?'

Jud glanced casually over at the pines and shrugged. 'Hell, that don't mean anything. He holds on to shit like it's money!'

Appreciative chuckles mingled with the repetitive thumping of axes. Perhaps it was because Waylan hadn't started using his that he was the first to pick up on the strange birdcall in the trees. His spine tingled as he glanced at Jud. 'It's a listening axe,' he finally answered, before bellowing at the whole detail, 'Defend yourselves!'

Jud stared at him in amazement, whilst Hoffman responded with indignation. 'I give zee orders here!'

At that moment a horrific apparition appeared at the tree line. Private Nelson, his government-issue trousers around his knees, staggered into view. Quite obviously a dead man walking, an arrow had transfixed his neck and his long johns were soaked with blood.

'Well bleedin' give some then,' Slade yelled at the startled corporal. 'The bastards are coming through the trees.' With that, the big man grabbed his Spencer and raced for the wagons.

With the abrupt cessation of work, everyone could hear the sound of unshod hoofs approaching at speed. The horsemanship required to rapidly pass through the forest was truly astounding. Charlie and Taylor instinctively closed in on Waylan as the three men followed their new 'friend'. The four civilians reached the makeshift barricade before the others and so witnessed the awesome sight of the Sioux warriors emerging from the forest.

The half-naked horsemen swept into the clearing and ferociously slaughtered those fleeing men who had been furthest from the wagons. Their weapons were primitive — hand axes, clubs and arrows — but at close range and against terrified and disorganized fugitives they were devastating. Two civilians and three more soldiers died without even a shot being fired. One young Indian, consumed by bloodlust, eagerly dismounted to collect his trophy. Brandishing a skinning knife, he seized hold of a clump of greasy hair and with a savage cry sliced through lifeless flesh. Yet even as he triumphantly held up the scalp for all to see, Slade's Spencer crashed out and brutally ended his short life.

That shot was to be the first of many and signalled a change in the fighting. As the remaining soldiers reached the wagons, their corporal restored some kind of order. Obeying Hoffman's barked commands, they spread out in a semi-circle and took careful aim with their muzzle-loading Springfield rifles. The Sioux were advancing in two waves. Their plan was all too obvious.

As the first wave surged towards the waiting infantry, a remarkably disciplined volley thundered out across the clearing. Three horses and their riders tumbled to the ground and the charge momentarily stalled, but as planned the second wave sped through the gaps screaming exultantly. From past experience they knew that they had little more to fear than the occasional revolver.

As the shrieking Indians rapidly drew nearer, the 'blue-coats' good order began to dissipate. With sheer desperation, the sweating soldiers tore open their paper cartridges to pour powder and Minie balls down rifled barrels. Next came ramrods and percussion caps. It all took far too long, and their actions were hampered by the awful knowledge that they wouldn't be in time. As the thundering horde drew closer, one terrified private levelled his rifle with the ramrod still in the barrel. There was merely a dull click as the hammer dropped on an empty nipple, the essential percussion cap still in its case. Only then did it suddenly dawn on him that they were all going to die!

3

But possibly not that day, because Waylan and his companions had faced cavalry before and *they* weren't equipped with out-dated muzzle-loaders. Safe in the knowledge that reloading wasn't an issue, they held off until the Sioux were almost up to the barricade and then opened fire. Three Henry rifles and a Spencer carbine crashed out, and then, to the Indians utter horror, kept on firing. Working the lever actions with practised speed, the white men sent an accurate stream of hot lead tearing through flesh and blood. There seemed to be no escape from the terrifying new weapons, and almost immediately the confident charge came to an abrupt end. As frightened riderless horses flowed around the circle of wagons, the surviving warriors turned and fled.

Those in the first wave stared in stunned

amazement as their comrades swarmed back towards them. The carefully planned attack had fallen apart and the rout was hastened when the 'blue coats' unleashed another volley from their Springfields. This time none of the Indians had any inclination to try and gamble on their opponents' reloading times. They simply joined the retreating second wave and raced for the trees.

The defenders were wreathed in black powder smoke, but they all recognized that something special had occurred. For a start, they were still alive. As blessed relief washed over them, some of the men began to hurl foul insults at the disappearing Indians, whilst another simply burst into tears. As Hoffman began to restore some discipline, Waylan suddenly became aware that Slade's eyes were boring into him.

'That was some real fancy shooting from you fellas,' the big man remarked. He sounded calm and completely unruffled by the bloody violence. 'I'm gonna have to get me one of those. I hear tell there's a new model just out called a Winchester. It must be really something.'

Killing folks had never come easily to Waylan. It had always left him feeling kind of empty inside. Consequently, he merely nodded non-committedly as he carefully slid fresh cartridges into the tubular magazine of his rifle. Reloading a Henry was not *that* simple, as it had to be done from the muzzle end.

It was Charlie Pickett who put the question that was on everyone's lips. 'So what happens now?'

Slade grunted. 'Way I see it, there's two choices. Either somebody goes for help, or we sit here and hope that they heard that ruckus back at the fort.' He suddenly laughed and called over to the nearest soldier. 'You know something? Those museum pieces are gonna get you blue bellies kilt one of these days, and I don't want to be there when it happens!'

The soldier glanced at him sourly. 'You're all heart, mister.'

Corporal Hoffman, making his way around the defenders, overheard that last exchange. He glared at the big civilian. 'Ve manage veil enough vithout you men. My report vill show that you merely assisted in ze defence.'

Slade reacted to that like an angry bull. 'The hell it will,' he roared, the veins on his thick neck standing out. 'But for us and these repeaters, you'd all be buzzard bait right now. Or else hanging from a lodge pole with your pecker in your mouth!'

Waylan regarded him curiously. For someone who supposedly knew nothing about such matters, he seemed to be very well informed. Before Hoffman could make any retort, a cry went up further round the perimeter. 'Those devils are on the move again, corporal!'

Sure enough, just visible beyond the tree line, a body of horsemen was weaving its way to another position. The Sioux were very deliberately splitting their forces.

Taylor Johnston rarely said anything, but when he did it was invariably worth listening to. 'They ain't finished with us yet,' he remarked earnestly. 'They're going to attack from two sides to thin out our defence and try to overwhelm us. It's what J.E.B. Stuart would have done, God rest his soul.'

It was obvious that some of the men hearing that didn't care for such talk, but Slade didn't give them a chance to comment. Spitting at the corporal's feet, he barked out, 'So what are your orders, *general*? Or do you want us *mere* civilians to sit this one out?'

Charlie Pickett sniggered in appreciation. He welcomed any opportunity to belittle the hated Yankees. The German non-com gritted his teeth angrily. Under different circumstances he would not have tolerated such behaviour. As it was, he did his best to save face. 'You must pick your own ground, ya? For it is also *your* pecker at risk, is it not?'

Anxious to diffuse the situation, Waylan smiled. 'You got that right, corporal.' Patting Slade gently on his massive shoulders, he suggested, 'What say you and I help cover the back door?'

As if to emphasize the good sense in that, howls of derision suddenly broke out on two sides of the clearing. The Sioux were again on the move, only this time they were making straight for the wagons. As Taylor had foreseen, both groups were attacking simultaneously, so that the defenders had no choice other than to fight on two fronts. As the Indians came on at a flat gallop, Slade and Waylan were joined by eight soldiers and one of the civilian woodcutters.

'You fellas have done this before, haven't you?' a young private queried nervously. His face was coated with sweat and one eyelid twitched involuntarily.

Waylan smiled reassuringly. 'It was a different war and a different enemy, but yeah we've done it before. So you just keep firing and reloading as fast as you can and we'll make sure nothing happens to you.'

Under such circumstances it was one hell of a promise, but nevertheless it had the effect of steadying the man's nerves. With new determination, he advanced to the barricade. Levelling their rifles, the soldiers unleashed a ragged broadside and then reached for fresh cartridges. Even as they did so, another volley crashed out behind them. The members of Hoffman's squad were now also fighting for their lives.

It was then that the three civilians opened fire, but they managed merely one round apiece before only Slade and Waylan remained. Their companion had taken a barbed arrow in his throat and was now choking to death on the grass beside them.

'That stockade just ain't ever gonna get built,' Slade yelled, as he cocked his Spencer for another shot.

This time the Sioux knew exactly what they were up against and so a few fatalities did not deter them. As they swarmed towards the circled wagons, screaming out their war cry 'Hoka hey, Hoka hey', Waylan worked his Henry like a man possessed. Quite deliberately, he aimed at the horses. They were not only the larger targets, but by bringing them down he also helped to break up the charge. His tactic worked. Impeded by their own fallen animals, the frustrated Indians separated like the tide on a breakwater. But they didn't retreat. Instead, a number of them swept around the sides and with amazing horsemanship made it through the narrow gaps between the wagons. Howling with bloodlust, they leapt upon the defenders.

Suddenly the circle's interior descended into chaos. The army's horses already in there milled around in terror, but had nowhere to go. The soldiers had managed to reload their Springfields, but no longer had the opportunity to use them. The battle had deteriorated into desperate hand-to-hand combat.

Possessing weapons of shorter barrel length, Slade and Waylan stood side by side and maintained a lethal fire at their opponents. No one could get close to them, and so instead a lean, muscular warrior gripping a bloodied tomahawk, leapt towards the nervous young private. That individual's eyes widened with horror as he regarded the visceral weapon.

Recalling his rash assurance, the southerner instinctively swung away to take a hand in the confrontation, thereby leaving himself open to attack. As the soldier frantically attempted to parry the axe blow, Waylan fired. His bullet struck the Indian just above the left hip, causing him to stagger sideways with shock. Suddenly emboldened by Waylan's intervention, the young recruit surged forward and swung his rifle butt in a great roundhouse blow. His saviour never did see the result.

Abruptly thrust sideways with tremendous force, Waylan tumbled back into the nearest wagon. Even as he did so, a lance tip pierced the planking next to him. Then, through blurred vision, he made out a paint-daubed warrior rushing towards him clutching a vicious-looking blade. Although partially stunned by the impact, the white man instinctively pumped the lever of his rifle and fired . . . only to be rewarded with a dull click. In the heat of action he had not noticed that the magazine's toggle had reached bottom.

His opponent's obsidian eyes flashed with triumph, as that man recognized Waylan's defenceless state — still groggy, he simply didn't have the co-ordination to reach for another weapon. As the knifepoint flashed towards him, a bloody and painful death loomed. The desperate fighting around him counted for nothing as he stared helplessly at his nemesis.

As if from nowhere, a gun butt slammed home with skull-crushing force, ensuring that the Indian would fall and never rise again. But that sure knowledge didn't stop Slade landing blow after sickening blow for good measure. Only when his blood lust was finally sated did he glance over at the young southerner.

'Looks like you ain't the only one out of rimfires,' he commented with remarkable composure. 'But then there's more than one way to skin a cat.' He paused momentarily, before adding with great emphasis, 'Reckon I just saved your life, mister. He was aiming to wash his hands in your brains!'

★　★　★

The short, ferociously fought battle was over and the white men had survived . . . but only just!

The remaining warriors had disappeared into the forest to lick their wounds and mourn their dead. But for the blood-soaked corpses strewn around the glade, the Sioux might not have ever been there, because after the cacophony of noise, what seemed like an eerie silence had settled over the circled wagons. It was broken only by the pathetic moans of the wounded.

Both Charlie and Taylor had survived unscathed. With two Henrys spitting defiance, the Indians had been unable to penetrate on their front. Not that Corporal Hoffman was even then prepared to acknowledge that their contribution had tipped the balance. He was obviously 'bucking' for promotion and keen to claim the victory as his own. So much so that he had no intention of waiting for a relief column.

'Hook up ze animals,' he ordered. 'Ve collect the wounded and go. I have much to report.'

That was altogether too much for Slade. He seemed to loathe Hoffman more than he did the Indians, and yet the big man also talked sense. 'Now wait just a God-damn minute, *general*. How d'you know those heathens have really gone? You haven't sent out any skirmishers. They could be up in those trees right now, watching and waiting. If they catch us on the move, we're finished. *Kaput*. Understand?'

A fresh flush of colour flooded the non-com's face, but before he could answer, Waylan added his 'ten cents' worth. 'I reckon he's right, corporal,' he announced in a more soothing, even tone. 'They *must* have heard all that shooting back at the fort. Far better to wait for a relief column to screen our retreat.'

No Prussian militarist worth his salt could stomach such intervention. In a strangely high-pitched tone, Hoffman yelled back, 'Zis is not a retreat. Ve haf von a great victory and ve need no help from ze colonel. You vill . . . '

What he was about to say was drowned out by a great cheer from the survivors. Waylan had been correct. The fight *had* been heard and Carrington had sent out reinforcements. In the lead was a badly under-strength troop of the 2nd Cavalry, followed some way back by a sweating company of infantry maintaining a punishing pace. The force's commander, Captain Brown, reined in and surveyed the carnage before him. His sharp eyes missed little and he soon arrived at certain conclusions.

'Seems like you had quite a fight on your hands, corporal. I'll wager you were damn glad of those repeaters.' Before the flustered non-com could respond, the officer added, 'You did right to stay put. Those devils would have overrun you for sure if you'd tried to make a break for it!'

★   ★   ★

Darkness had finally fallen on a very eventful day, but it brought with it little respite. Pitch torches flamed around the perimeter of Fort Phil Kearny. The guard had been doubled, and word was out that Colonel Carrington feared that an all-out attack on his post was highly likely. With the howitzers' power negated by the gloom and a stockade that was only partially built around them, sleep eluded even those off duty. Waylan and his friends sat around a campfire with their new companion. Unlike the previous night, their conversation was low, restrained, and completely lacking in humour. Slade had come to a stark conclusion and he wasn't keeping it to himself.

'The Sioux have cut up rough before, but nothing like this. Red Cloud wants all the forts on the Bozeman destroyed. He's out for blood, and if we're not careful it could be ours.' He paused and glanced scornfully at the prowling sentries. 'Because I'll tell you one thing for sure, these sons of bitches know doodly-squat about fighting Indians.'

The others regarded him intently. As expected, it was Waylan who asked the obvious question. 'So what are you suggesting?' Then he, too, also paused, as something else occurred to him. 'And how come you know so much about the frontier and its people?'

Slade sneered. 'They ain't *people*. They're just savages. But I'll allow, they do know how to make war. It's in their blood.' He still hadn't answered either of Waylan's queries. All he had offered so far was bitterness and prejudice, but that was about to change. After glancing suspiciously around, he leaned in closer to the fire and continued with, 'We need to get out of here while we still can. Wait 'til the small hours, when everyone's settled down some. Then we saddle our horses and lead them out quietly. There ain't enough guards to cover the whole perimeter all the time, and besides . . . they're watching for folks with bows and arrows coming in, not us going out. Once we get clear of the fort, we shouldn't have any Indian trouble for a while. Red Cloud's boys are crowding the blue bellies like ticks on a Texas steer.'

Charlie's eyes widened in surprise. How the hell did Slade know about Texas ticks?

'Seems like you've got it all worked out,' Taylor remarked warily. 'But won't that make us deserters?'

'From what?' Slade scoffed. 'I don't know about you, but I ain't put my mark to any paper. Way I see it, we're only here 'cause Carrington took it upon his self to close the trail . . . but if Red Cloud chooses to ignore that, then why can't we? And I reckon that high an' mighty colonel will have too much on his mind to bother sending out after us.'

As usual it was Waylan who spoke decisively for the southerners. 'In a free country, no man's got good reason to impose himself on others. Yet it happened in the war and it's still happening now. Just 'cause they won, don't make it right! We saved their skins this afternoon and got little thanks for it, so I'm for leaving.'

The others studied him intently. Slade had a half-smile on his face and was nodding agreement. It was Charlie Pickett who put his seal on the idea. 'Virginia City here we come, and the devil take anyone who tries to stop us!'

That would prove to be an unfortunately prophetic remark.

*   *   *

As Slade had anticipated, with the night progressing without any further contact by the Sioux, the sentries began to lose their heightened alertness. Boredom set in and their vigilance deteriorated. Yawning, the soldiers no longer patrolled the whole perimeter. The four conspirators deliberately let their fire burn out, so that when the time came they could move off unobserved. And that time had arrived.

Slade gestured towards the corral and got to his feet. Since it had been his idea, the southerners were giving him his head. Clutching their weapons and saddles, they followed him closely. The four men reached the enclosure without attracting a challenge. One or two of the animals snickered curiously but remained quiet. The big man opened the gate and then uncharacteristically stepped aside to let the others enter. The night seemed to swallow him whole as he temporarily disappeared from view. It was now, while they located and saddled their horses, that the deserters were most vulnerable.

'Vas ist dies?' The instantly recognizable voice seemed to come out of nowhere. It was accompanied by the metallic sound of a revolver being cocked. The three young men watched with abject dismay as Corporal Hoffman emerged from the gloom. His normally sour features displayed unmistakable triumph, backed up by the levelled weapon in his right hand. The non-com tilted his head slightly, as though about to summon the guard. His intended words would never be known though, because at that moment Waylan detected movement behind the other man's back.

Slade's huge form appeared, so that he suddenly dwarfed the unsuspecting soldier. His left arm enveloped Hoffman's neck in a vice-like grip, whilst his right hand closed over the revolver. With a thick forefinger deliberately wedged between the hammer and percussion cap, he yanked it effortlessly out of the corporal's grasp and tossed it over to Waylan. That man deftly caught it and very carefully lowered the hammer.

It was then, when the moment of greatest danger had passed, that events took a very dark turn. With Hoffman struggling helplessly against Slade's overwhelming strength, all it needed was a blow to the head to subdue him. Instead, a naked blade abruptly appeared in Slade's hand. Simultaneously, as he favoured the horrified southerners with a beaming grin, he plunged it deep into his victim's belly. Even though half-throttled, there was no containing the strangled groan that escaped that man's lips. The hapless soldier thrashed around like a dying fish, until Slade again thrust his honed steel in and then viciously twisted it.

Even in the inky darkness, the horrified spectators couldn't miss the glistening blood that now drenched Hoffman's jacket. As the assassin carefully lowered his lifeless body to the ground, he couldn't resist a soft chuckle.

'One thing's for sure,' Slade remarked. 'There won't be no one calling him *blue* belly after this night's work!'

Waylan's face was akin to a mask as he advanced on the bear-like killer. Underneath, he was seething with anger, but this was not the time for that. So when they were almost nose-to-nose, he merely remarked, 'There was no need for that.' If he had been expecting any sign of contrition he would have been sadly disappointed.

'There was every need,' Slade hissed. 'He had it coming, and besides . . . I enjoyed it!'

For a long, tense moment the two men stared at each other. Then Taylor interrupted and the urgency in his voice was unmistakable. 'Sweet Jesus, fellas. We just ain't got time for this. If we didn't *have* to leave before, we sure as hell do now.'

That broke the spell. Waylan and Slade moved apart and all four men wordlessly saddled their mounts. Without any further interruptions, they were soon leading them out beyond the intended limits of the fort and across Big Piney Creek. All four of the fugitives, which of course was what they now were, had obtained little sleep since the previous night, but they had to get well clear of Phil Kearny before first light. Waylan fervently hoped that, under the circumstances, the colonel might have far more on his mind than the capture of four white renegades, but a niggling doubt told him that he was being over-optimistic.

4

Daybreak found the now unemployed loggers a few miles to the north-west. During the remaining hours of darkness they had made careful progress and had not encountered a soul. It seemed as though Slade had been right. The Sioux warriors were congregating around Fort Phil Kearny, leaving the trail itself a surprisingly safe place. And yet, rather than continue, Waylan decided to call a halt. Something was gnawing on him that needed addressing, and even the stunning scenery could not distract him. Off to their left, on higher ground, was a sizeable stand of trees with the Bighorn Mountains looming spectacularly in the background.

'This will serve,' he announced, affecting not to notice the curious look on Slade's face.

Dismounting, the four men led their

animals into the trees. With no visible clearing and the wood seemingly deserted, Waylan nevertheless drew and cocked his Colt Army revolver. The muzzle settled on one particular individual and prompted an immediate response from the huge man.

'Seems to me you've got something sticking in your craw, young fella.'

The southerner nodded emphatically. 'God knows I've got no love for Yankee soldiers, but I don't hold with cold-blooded murder and neither do my friends. You could have just cold-cocked that corporal and they'd have likely just lost interest in us, what with the Indian trouble an' all. As it is, whatever you said before, I believe they'll definitely pursue us now.'

Slade regarded the Colt with apparent calm. 'So where's this leading?'

Waylan glanced at his friends and they both nodded their agreement. 'We split up now and you go your own separate path, as if we never met. And that way, if we are followed, there'll be two sets of tracks to make life harder for them.'

'Just like that,' the other man bristled. 'Me saving your life an' all don't amount to a hill of beans. Is that it?'

The young man sighed regretfully. He'd known this wasn't going to be easy. 'That's not true,' he avowed. 'I owe you a huge debt and maybe some day I'll be able to repay it. But not here and not now. I guess you and I just see things differently and that means we're not right for each other.' A chill crept into his voice as he added sharply, 'Now get moving!'

Slade stared at him for a moment and then laughed out loud. His surprising response was suddenly coated with menace. 'Or else what? You'll gut me like a fish? I don't think so. Like you said, you don't hold with cold-blooded murder. No, sonny boy, I reckon you and me is stuck with each other. At least until we get out of Indian territory.'

Waylan stared at him, temporarily lost for words. He hadn't expected such a response and so it was left to Taylor to make the running. Ostentatiously cocking his Henry, he too pointed it directly at their erstwhile 'friend'. 'Charlie and me ain't beholden to you for nothing and we travel where we please and with who we please. So either you git and stay git or we'll do the cold-cocking and truss you up like a turkey for good measure. What'll it be, mister?'

Slade's jaw noticeably tightened, as he coldly regarded Waylan's friends. He recognized the determination etched on Taylor's dark features, backed up by the eagerness on Charlie's, and finally uttered a deep sigh.

'So that's how it is. Well, I'll tell you, fellas, I'm right disappointed in you. Didn't think to mention it before, but I've been looking for men that are good with a gun and you boys definitely make the grade. You're throwing up a real fine opportunity to draw some top dollar in Virginia City and live high for maybe the first time in your lives.'

He regarded them silently for a

moment, waiting to see if their curiosity had been aroused. When no response was forthcoming, he shook his head regretfully. 'Well, you've thrown it back at me and being as this is no time or place for a shooting dispute, I guess I'll just have to bow out and be on my way.' So saying, he pulled on his horse's reins and headed back out of the trees. 'I'll leave you something else to think on though. If Carrington does decide he wants Hoffman's killer, I reckon I know who he'll send. A hombre name of Jim Bridger!'

The name meant nothing to the young men. Charlie shook his head in bewilderment. 'And just who the hell is he?'

Pausing, Slade half-turned and favoured him with a chilling smile. 'Ain't never had a run-in with him myself, but I hear tell he's an ornery old bastard, who knows the frontier like the back of his hand. In fact, the only thing he don't know is when to quit. And if you're giving me the road, then happen he'll find you first. So enjoy. Ha ha ha!'

★ ★ ★

In addition to laying claim to a very unusual name, Colonel Henry Beebee Carrington also possessed the undeniably grand title of Commander of the Mountain District, Department of the Platte. Sadly he seemed to derive little joy from his position. From the moment of his arrival in the Powder River Country he had been plagued by problems, most of them involving extremely hostile Indians. But as if that wasn't sufficient, he now had to deal with the murder of a non-commissioned officer by white men. It really was enough to make God weep!

Standing before him were three men . . . or rather two. Captain Brown, as befitted an officer, sat to one side nursing a mug of coffee. His brow furrowed with each sip. The only civilian in the headquarters tent hinted as to the reason for that.

'God damn! This coffee's strong enough to float a pistol,' he exclaimed.

Carrington offered a thin smile, which

did little to banish the anxiety from his drawn features. 'I'm glad it's to your liking, Mister Bridger. Now, if we can get to business. There are many pressing demands on my time.'

'Talk away, Colonel. You've got my full attention,' Bridger responded amiably. It had been a long time, if ever, since he had been in awe of a smart uniform. Now aged over sixty, Jim Bridger was a legend on the frontier, if only because he had managed to retain his scalp for so long. As far back as the 1820s he had been an employee of the Rocky Mountain Fur Company. Since then he had been an explorer, hunter, trader and lately a scout for the US Army. He was gnarled, arthritic, and tough as old boots.

'Four civilian loggers brutally murdered Corporal Hoffman last night and then fled. I want them found and brought back for trial.'

Bridger's leathery skin seemed almost to creak as he fixed his gaze on Carrington. 'You sure they weren't fleeing anyway and Hoffman just got in the way?'

The colonel snorted dismissively. '*Whatever* reasons they had, can't excuse their actions. I want those killers apprehended. Unfortunately, because of what also took place yesterday, I've got a blockhouse to construct near the pinery and so I can only spare you one man.'

A stubborn set came over Bridger's features. 'Can't argue with that, Colonel. Those logging details of yours draw Indians like flies to fresh shit, but I *ain't* taking some young snot nose with me, no sir. It's dangerous country hereabouts and I'll need him to watch my back.'

Carrington gestured at the fourth man in the tent. 'I'm well aware of that fact. That's why Sergeant Rudabauer here will accompany you. He will be in charge of all military aspects of this mission. Also, he knows what all four of the fugitives look like, which I'll wager is more than you do.'

Bridger glanced at the veteran noncom and favoured him with a genuinely warm smile. 'I can live with that,' he replied.

Rudabauer stiffened as he regarded his commanding officer. 'Permission to speak, sir?'

'Granted.'

'Three of those fellas were southerners, so they held no love for us bluecoats, but I didn't take them for cold-blooded killers. They were just heading for Virginia City to try their luck panning for gold. For my money it would be the one called Slade. He had the look.'

Captain Brown spoke for the first time. 'I agree with the sergeant, sir. From what I saw yesterday, I believe those three made a real difference with their Henry repeaters. In fact I reckon we owe them more than just a rope.'

Carrington grunted. Other worries were crowding his thoughts and he was rapidly losing interest in the matter. 'That will be for me to ascertain at a later date. For now, you know the direction they have likely taken, so I just want them *all* caught. Dismissed!'

Completely ignoring the mixture of tents and hastily erected wooden buildings of which the settlement mostly comprised, Henry Plummer gazed eagerly down the muddy thoroughfare towards the northeast. It was from that direction that the circuitous Bozeman Trail finally made its way across the Flathead River and on into the grandiosely titled Virginia City. As on every morning for the past few days, he was oblivious to the gaze of curious passers-by because he was watching for a very particular new arrival. A man who knew more about killing and intimidation than anyone else he'd ever met. A man who would help him turn around the particularly dire situation that he now found himself in, and who would hopefully be accompanied by like-minded individuals keen to earn big money. Of course, for anybody enquiring about his anxious vigil, he also had a very legitimate reason. His saloon's whiskey supply was running low.

As many people had found out to their cost, Plummer was a dark and complex character. In addition to running Virginia City's largest saloon, he was also the leader of a dwindling gang of 'road agents' known as the Innocents. They came about this remarkably optimistic name on account of their password, when challenged, being 'I am innocent'.

His gang was dwindling because the prospectors and businessmen inhabiting the gold field in Alder Gulch had, not unnaturally, got tired of being robbed and murdered. In a region devoid of any law and order, they had enlisted their own band of vigilantes, with the equally colourful name of 'Stuart's Stranglers'. Led by Granville Stuart, the Stranglers lynched any man even suspected of wrong-doing, and such a policy was taking its toll on the Innocents. It was only by taking great care that Plummer had managed to avoid suspicion falling on himself. He also suspected that Stuart had an agenda of his own, which included taking control of the settlement to further his own ends. A power struggle seemed inevitable.

After remaining motionless for many minutes, he spat a stream of yellow phlegm into the nearest puddle. 'God damn it all to hell! Why don't he come? Why don't *anybody* come?'

Everyone in the mining camp had noticed that traffic on the Bozeman Trail had abruptly ceased. Something mighty serious had to have occurred to halt the flow of eager prospectors and freighters bringing supplies. Dime to a dollar those tarnal redskins had something to do with it. Unhappily turning away, Plummer trudged back through the ever-present mud to the Top Saloon. Although very spacious and possessing an ambitious false front, the building was little more than a single-storey, clapboard structure, offering very little of the promise that its name suggested. And yet his ownership of it projected the illusion that he was merely a genuine businessman, as well as providing a lucrative income and access to all the news in the camp.

As the swarthy saloon-keeper entered his dingy premises, he bellowed out, 'Whiskey, and bring the bottle!'

A short while later, sitting at his personal table in the half-light at the rear of the main room, he came to a decision. It behoved him, as one of the founders of the prospecting community that he so avidly preyed upon, to find out just what was happening beyond the city's limits. A rider would have to be sent through the Bozeman Pass to investigate. The task would require someone of moderate intelligence, rational judgement, and the ability to act on his own initiative. Sadly, none of his employees possessed any of those qualities, so he would just have to make do.

'Wendell, get yourself over here,' Plummer barked out.

The individual who approached him was a bovine brute of a man. Although of only average height, Wendell Storey was built like a house-side. He had a slick of black, greasy hair and a knife scar that ran the length of his right cheek. The only reason that he had not been lynched was because his boss had deliberately kept him clear of any thieving. Storey belonged exclusively to the Top Saloon, and helped ensure that its rowdier elements did not overstay their welcome. The huge Colt Dragoon revolver habitually tucked into his belt further added to his allure.

As Plummer explained what was required, Storey's face fell. He did not like horses and they did not like him, but nevertheless he knew that he would have to comply. Despite his own massive bulk and violent tendencies, there was something about his employer that had always made him nervous. He well knew that the saloon-keeper was adept at using cold steel to enforce his word. Up close and personal. The kind of blood-letting that really made you *feel* your victim's pain.

'Remember,' instructed the saloon-keeper, 'If you cross paths with any law dogs or army, you're only there to find out what's happened to our supplies.

But if you do meet Slade and his men, you lead him back here, pronto. They're the real reason you're out there. And try not to kill anyone that you don't have to,' Plummer added hopefully.

Storey grunted and lumbered off out of the saloon without a word. It occurred to his slow mind that it might be best to stay on his horse and just keep on going, away from Henry Plummer and all his dark deeds. There was only one problem with that. By himself, he always seemed to end up in trouble, and besides . . . he really didn't have anywhere else to go.

Plummer glanced around his domain, taking in the habitual drinkers whose only aim in life was to pan a few flakes of gold and then exchange them for cheap trader whiskey. Then his hard eyes settled on one particular customer who just didn't look right in such a 'piss pit' at that hour of the day, and he stiffened in his chair. The saloon-keeper thought he could recognize a 'Strangler' when he saw one, and the possibility made his

64

blood boil. That he should actually be under surveillance in his own premises! It showed that he was now considered to be a suspect. He suddenly itched to utilize the knife secreted in his left boot, but knew that the time wasn't right. A blatant murder would only confirm their suspicions and he was short on hired help. If only Slade would fetch up with some prime gunhands, his days of having to tolerate such things would be over. After all, in a town without law and order, it was the man with the biggest stick who would come out on top.

★   ★   ★

'Perhaps we should have stayed together a bit longer,' Charlie muttered unhappily.

Waylan stared at him in astonishment. 'Not so long ago, you were all for beating on him.'

'Yeah, yeah, I know. Only I've been thinking about that other fort up ahead. We don't even know where it is, and

Slade seemed to know his way about this neck of the woods. This trail's supposed to be closed to all civilians, so we could be stopped again. Only this time we might be wanted for murder. And then there was that bit about earning top dollar. What was all that about?'

It was plain that Charlie had been doing some unaccustomed deep thinking and wasn't enjoying the result. The three friends had remained in the wood, to rest up and give Slade time to move on, but the respite hadn't lightened their mood any. And with the knowledge that pursuit was highly likely, it really was time to get moving.

'The telegraph hasn't reached out this far yet, so nobody up ahead is going to know about Hoffman,' Taylor responded with considered reasoning. 'So all we need to do is . . . ' His mouth closed like a trap as he caught sight of a small band of horsemen suddenly visible on the trail below.

The newcomers were half-naked, sun-bronzed and completely unaware that they were being watched. Riding their ponies as though born to it and with strung bows canted across the withers of their mounts, even at a distance the warriors projected an air of menace. Even so, their unexpected presence would not have mattered had it not been for their direction of travel: north-west!

As Taylor's startled companions followed his gaze, they all reacted in the same way. Moving swiftly over to the horses, their hands closed around the animals' jaws, ensuring that the creatures did not inadvertently give away their position. With the Indians unsuspectingly continuing on their way, it was Waylan who highlighted the dilemma facing himself and his friends.

'We're between a rock and a hard place now, an' no mistake. We can't wait around here much longer, because if this Bridger is as good as Slade reckons, he'll find us in these trees for sure. And yet we don't know what those sons of bitches are up to either. If they were to call a halt, we could stumble into them without knowing it and there'd be hell to pay.'

'And what about Slade?' Charlie queried. 'What if they overhaul him down the road? We sent him off on his lonesome and that Spencer's not up to taking them all on.'

'Don't you think I don't know that?' Waylan responded bitterly. 'It was my life he saved in that bloodbath!' He paused for a moment to ponder the situation, but in truth he already knew the answer. 'We've no choice but to follow on. And we'll have to keep all our wits about us. As though Robert E. Lee himself is watching us. Because from now on, we'll likely have enemies both in front and behind. Savvy?'

His two companions nodded grimly. Oh, they savvied all right!

5

The two men had slipped out of Fort Phil Kearny shortly after the noisy departure of the logging detail. Jim Bridger correctly reasoned that the daily procession of rattling wagons was likely to have drawn off any Sioux in the area. After splashing through the creek, they had ridden cautiously up the trail for some hours in total silence. The ageing army scout had little time for small talk. His arthritic right hip was already beginning to ache, and in any case, he was fully occupied.

Bridger's sharp eyes relentlessly scanned the middle distance searching for any signs of life. Pretty much anything they were likely to encounter would be hostile. He was aided by Carrington's closure of the trail and the consequent lack of traffic and he had already spotted the separate tracks of shod and unshod hoofs.

Even though unlettered, he was still able to put two and two together.

Sergeant Rudabauer, unskilled in such matters, was oblivious to all this and was thoroughly unnerved by the civilian's stubborn silence. Finally he just couldn't take it any longer.

'Sweet Jesus,' he exclaimed softly. 'Don't you ever get the urge for a chinwag?'

A chill smile slowly spread across Bridger's weathered features, but even as he replied, his eyes continued to roam the terrain. 'You start to relax out here and you'll like as not lose your scalp. But I suppose if you've got questions, then happen I can accommodate you.'

The soldier glanced nervously at the clusters of trees on either side of the trail. For all he knew, they could be full of savages. He was out of his depth and sensible enough to recognize the fact. And talking did help.

'Thought you'd be carrying a fifty calibre Hawken or some such. I heard tell that was a mountain man's favourite rifle.'

Despite the situation, Bridger chuckled. 'Nah,' he responded, patting the stock of his Sharps Rifle. 'I've moved with the times.' Then his eyes momentarily settled on the sergeant. 'You really have no idea what's ahead of us, do you?'

The other man blinked rapidly in a nervous reaction. 'Say what?'

Bridger sighed and tugged his horse to a stop. 'Well I guess you need to know, since you're supposed to be in charge of this detail. Our runaways had a falling out in a grove of trees back down the trail a ways. One went off on his lonesome, followed by a band of hostiles. Then the other three white men went after them, but of course the Indians will know that. They'd been following all four of them for some time and knew about their detour. Now I reckon they'll be laying in wait for them up ahead somewhere.'

Rudabauer's jaw quite literally dropped. 'How the hell can you know all this? All I see is an empty trail.'

For the first time that day, Bridger's

features crinkled into a warm grin. 'That's why the US Army pays me sixty dollars and found each month. I reckon that's more than you get, huh?'

The non-com grimaced, but then glanced anxiously around them. 'Yeah, it damn well is, but if you can keep us alive out here then I reckon you're worth it.' He paused for a moment, as Bridger's astounding news sank in. 'So just what do we do about all this?'

For a brief moment, the scout focused all his attention on his companion. What he had to say was chilling in its simplicity. 'Leave them to fight it out and then move in and pick up the pieces. Them renegades murdered one of your boys, so they'll be no loss.'

The sergeant absorbed that in shocked silence. He knew that what the tough old scout said made good tactical sense, but that didn't make it right. Rudabauer was struggling to overcome a strong desire for self-preservation and he only just managed it.

'Well I'm right sorry to cross you,

Jim,' he reluctantly announced. 'I surely am. But we can't do that. I reckon only one of those boys is a killer. The other three helped save the logging detail and just want to pan for some gold. They ain't even deserters really, because they never even signed on.'

Bridger squinted at him in surprise. 'That's just a piece of pure foolishness. I haven't survived into my fifth decade on the frontier by being soft in the head.' He suddenly favoured the soldier with an appraising glance. 'You know what a decade is, don't you?'

That was too much for Rudabauer. 'I can read, write and cipher, which I'll wager is more than you can. I also know this is army business and that makes it my decision. If you can't handle that, you'd best head back to the fort.'

Bridger calmly sat his horse and bit off a plug of tobacco. As the dark juice trickled over the stubble on his chin, he came to his own conclusion. 'You're a real push hard, ain't you? But I suppose you've got one thing right. It *is* army business. And I guess I'd better stick around, because let's face it, you'd be lost without me!'

That final comment was dramatically punctuated by a burst of gunfire further up the trail. Whatever else there was to say would definitely have to wait.

★   ★   ★

By rights, they should all have been dead. The ambush had been timed to perfection, and the only thing that had saved them was the known fact that Indians couldn't shoot worth a damn. Even so, the three friends were in big trouble. A fusillade of shots had opened up from both sides without warning. Charlie's horse had taken an arrow in its haunches and toppled sideways, in the process pinning his right leg underneath. The other two men, along with their animals, had reached a jumble of rocks at the side of the trail and tethered the reins under the heaviest they could lift. They could only hope that the Sioux valued the creatures enough as potential prizes to let them live, because there was nothing more that they could do to protect them. Even as the white men took cover, a ricochet cut into the soft flesh of Taylor's left ear and he howled with pain.

'Shit! That damn near took my ear off,' he exclaimed.

Waylan had greater concerns. 'Is your leg broke?' he yelled at Charlie.

'Cain't tell, but I guess there's one sure way to find out. Give me some covering fire.'

With bullets and arrows kicking up grass and dirt around him, he placed his left boot on the saddle and pressed hard. The poor animal was screaming with agony, but there could be no help for that until he got clear. With Waylan rapidly firing back at the puffs of smoke, Charlie ignored his own pain and twisted and pushed with all his might. Suddenly the limb pulled free and so now he would get his answer. Grabbing his rifle from its leather scabbard, he clambered to his feet and ran awkwardly to the rocks. His leg took the strain, just. It hurt like Hades, but no bones were broken.

'Whose God-damned idea was it to go prospecting, anyhu?' His raw anger was fuelled by more than just pain. With tears of emotion in his eyes, the young man turned and dispatched his suffering horse with a well-aimed head shot. 'Those heathen sons of bitches'll pay for this,' he snarled.

The only response was continued gunfire, and vicious stone chips flew through the air around them. All three men realized that their position was untenable. Hidden in the trees, the Indians held all the aces. They had a height advantage and even accuracy was no longer an issue because, so long as they had enough cartridges, sooner or later another ricochet was bound to strike flesh.

'There's nothing else for it,' Waylan abruptly announced, as he slid fresh cartridges into the magazine of his Henry. 'They'll cut us to pieces here. We'll have to take our chances and rush the Sioux on this side.'

Taylor was aghast. 'That's a plan?' Waylan ignored him and turned to Charlie. 'That's a steep slope and your leg will slow you down, so you'll give cover. Are you loaded?'

The other man fished some shells out of his pocket.

'One moment.'

Crouching low, under incessant fire from enemies that they hadn't even seen yet, his friends waited impatiently for him to finish. Instinctively, their eyes met. This was truly desperate and both knew that they might not survive, but it certainly wasn't the first such occasion in their young lives. Then, as though deliberately testing their resolve, a cacophony of whoops and howls sounded off in the wooded hills around them. It was almost as though their opponents knew what was coming next.

Finally the magazine was capped off. 'Ready,' Charlie fatefully announced, as he glanced at Waylan for the word of command.

The deeper crash of a heavier

weapon was not what any of them were expecting. During their brief time at the fort, they had been told that in addition to their traditional weapons, the Indians possessed a mixture of old trader muskets and a few modern repeating rifles. This was something different.

The fire from the trees before them abruptly ceased and Waylan had a hunch. 'Fire at those bastards behind us,' he yelled at Charlie. 'I think we've already got some kind of help over here.' With that, he leapt to his feet and powered up the slope, zigzagging as he went.

Even as he and Taylor closed in on the treeline, they heard more firing from off to their right. Finally, with their chests heaving fit to burst, the two men reached the pines. Sure enough, two bronzed bodies lay on the ground, blood pumping from mortal wounds. With the tables lethally turned, the three remaining warriors were desperately searching for the source of the sudden death that had assailed them. Now, with two more white men in their rear, they recognized that their medicine had turned irreparably bad.

Even as Waylan and Taylor breathlessly opened up with their Henrys, the Sioux turned and fled. Leaping on to their waiting ponies, they swiftly threaded a way through the trees. Just before they got out of sight, the heavy calibre rifle crashed out once more and the rearmost Indian was flung from his mount. And then, quite suddenly, it was all over!

Still sucking air into their lungs, the two southerners curiously searched for their saviour. They knew it couldn't be Slade, because whoever it was hadn't been using a Spencer. To their absolute amazement, a blue uniform came into view.

'Rudabauer,' they both exclaimed together.

The sergeant offered them a wry smile as he cautiously advanced. 'The very same,' he remarked. 'And here's the man that saved your miserable hides.'

From behind a broad tree, an apparently ancient civilian appeared. He was busily feeding a paper cartridge into the breech of his Sharps rifle and paid them absolutely no heed.

'We'd better check on your excitable friend,' Rudabauer stated. From the way he said it, it was a command rather than a suggestion, yet their gratitude was such that they thought nothing of it. They were bursting with questions, but it was not yet the time. Watchfully, the three men emerged from the trees. Amazingly, Charlie waved cheerfully up at them. He was no longer firing or under fire, and all of them could hear the sound of fast-moving ponies in the pines opposite.

'Seems like those varmints have had enough as well,' Rudabauer declared with evident relief, and together they scrambled down to the jumble of rocks, followed by Bridger's silent figure leading two horses. Charlie stared at him curiously, even as he greeted the 'bluecoat'.

'So it's you we have to thank for chasing off the Sioux.'

Before Rudabauer could answer,

Bridger's gravelly voice interrupted. 'Them's Cheyenne, *not* Sioux, you swimmy head. They don't always see eye to eye with each other, but they sure as hell hate us. I met with Black Horse and Dull Knife two moons back and they made that very plain.'

The three southerners stared at him in amazement, but their surprises were far from over.

By way of explanation, the non-com remarked, 'This here's Jim Bridger. He's a scout for Colonel Carrington.'

The stranger's name meant nothing to them, but the ominous double click of the sergeant's service revolver definitely caught their attention.

'We ain't just out here for our health. We're looking for you fellas. And now that we've found you, you'll oblige me by handing over all your shooting irons. Easy now,' he added, as he saw Charlie's eyes flash dangerously. 'Be kind of a shame to put a ball in you after saving your life . . . but if I have to, I will,' he added firmly.

'That's just plum crazy,' Taylor protested. 'Disarming us in Indian territory. What if we're attacked again?'

'You should have thought of that before you kilt Hoffman,' Bridger remarked coldly.

Waylan fairly bristled with anger. 'That wasn't us, mister. It was Slade. That's why we parted company. We're none of us murderers.'

Rudabauer sighed and then nodded his head understandingly. 'Son, I actually believe you. I really do. But the colonel, well he just goes about things in a straight line. I'm under orders to take all of you back to stand trial and I didn't get these stripes by disobeying officers. So you stay with us while we catch up with Slade and then we'll all of us go back to the fort together. If you're innocent, then you've got nothing to worry about. How's that sound?'

It didn't sound good at all, but before any of the *prisoners* had a chance to comment, Bridger added his own ten cents' worth. 'You boys can roll all your shooting irons up in this old blanket,' he instructed, untying the fly-blown article from behind his saddle. 'We get jumped by any more hostiles, you can have them back, pronto.' He chuckled drily. 'It's like we're keeping them on trust for you, ha ha.'

That was just too much for Charlie. 'You look like you've been out in the sun way too long, old man.'

'Maybe so, but I'll be here long after you've gone, sonny. Now do as the man says, before I do the world a favour and pop a cap on you.'

It was Rudabauer who broke the tension by stating the obvious. 'We can't stay here eyeballing each other. There's been a powerful lot of shooting that could bring other hostiles looking. Two of you will have to ride double . . . once you've handed over your guns.'

Waylan stared at him long and hard, before finally nodding. 'Do as he says, fellas. We ain't killed any Yankees *this* year and I ain't starting now.'

6

Henry Plummer's eyes snapped open in response to some sound that was out of the ordinary. He'd finally slept, yes, but for how long he'd no idea. As his eyes adjusted to the gloom, so the fog cleared from his brain. He realized that it must be late on in the day, because of the volume of noise coming from his premises. Business was obviously lucratively brisk. Then there was another sharp tap on the door and this time he was ready.

'What is it?' he hoarsely demanded.

Only then did Hezekiah enter the small room at the rear of the Top Saloon. The barkeeper had once thought to cross the threshold without giving notice and had nearly had his throat cut for the privilege.

'It's me, Mister Plummer,' he nervously announced as he closed the door behind him. 'You said you wanted to know if that fella came back. The one that didn't look right for this . . . place.'

'And?'

'Well that's the thing. He never actually left. He's been here all day, while you's been resting. I just thought you should know, is all.'

Light suddenly flared in the murk of the windowless space, as Plummer used a lucifer to ignite the kerosene lamp next to his bed. Only now that he could see his weasel-faced employee did he put the next question.

'What's he been doing all this time?'

'Working on a bottle of our finest.' The sarcasm that accompanied the statement was all too obvious, but in truth well placed.

'Has he been drinking it or just *sipping* it?'

Hezekiah regarded him warily. 'Sipping.'

The saloon owner grunted knowingly. 'So he's still sober, and for a reason. Time I found out what that is.

You see any others with him?'

His employee gave a pretty fair impression of concentrated thought before replying with, 'The Top's heaving tonight, boss. I don't recognize half of them. You know how it is. New men coming to the diggings all the time. The Bozeman's not the only route for prospectors.'

The other man stared at him for a moment before grunting and abruptly waving him away. 'Get back behind the bar and keep that sawn-off handy, but don't even think about using it without my say so. That big gun's a real crowd pleaser and I don't want to be anywhere in front of it if it goes off.'

As the door closed again on the din of raucous voices, Plummer pondered the situation. He didn't like surprises, because all those that he'd encountered in the past had invariably gone bad on him. After loosening the knife in his boot, he came to a decision and tucked a Colt Police Pocket revolver in the small of his back, underneath his jacket.

After cautiously stepping out of his

room, the saloon owner and sometime outlaw stood with his back to the door, carefully surveying his domain. Night had indeed fallen and the place was heaving with thirsty prospectors, eager to forget the long hours of backbreaking toil that was their lot. They brought with them excessive noise, lice and disagreeable odours: unpleasant attributes that were balanced by a welcome supply of gold flake and even the occasional nugget. The large but basic premises were lit by a mixture of candles and oil lamps, with the result that illumination came in uneven patterns.

The customer of particular interest to him had moved to a corner table, so that he had no blind side and was mostly in shadow. What was especially striking was the fact that even though there was great demand, the tables immediately near the stranger remained empty, thereby consigning him to deliberate isolation: although that didn't necessarily mean that he was *completely* alone. And doubtless he was armed, but his long frockcoat hampered specific confirmation of the fact.

After casting a quick glance over at Hezekiah, Plummer did what was undoubtedly expected of him and walked steadily over to join the stranger. Alert to everything around him, he could feel an uncomfortable band of tension tighten around his chest. The other man suddenly kicking a chair out towards him didn't help that condition any.

'Join me,' came the abrupt invitation. 'You know you want to.'

The voice was cool, measured, and strangely cultured, and somehow gave the impression that everything about this meeting had been pre-planned. Plummer was also assailed by the uncomfortable notion that he was merely a visitor in his own premises. It was only when seated that he got his first proper look at the man who had unaccountably idled away a whole day in the seedy establishment. What he saw wasn't encouraging. The stranger possessed a face like a hatchet: lean, unusually clean-shaven and containing the coldest eyes that the saloon-keeper had ever locked on to. The short diatribe that followed was obviously well prepared, but no less chilling because of it.

'I've deliberately passed the whole day in this shit hole to get your attention and to make you realise that my intentions are serious. I'm a serious man, with serious matters to discuss. Should you forget that, it will go badly for you. Savvy?'

Despite his unease, Plummer felt a surge of anger. He'd just been threatened in his own place, and simply couldn't let that stand. His right hand began to drift down towards the knife in his boot. The furtive movement didn't go unnoticed.

'Don't be a fool, Mister *Innocent*. The Stranglers know all about your activities. The only reason you're still breathing is because they need you for something . . . special.'

A great chill enveloped Henry Plummer. If only he hadn't sent Wendell Storey off on an errand. The Colt tucked in his waistband suddenly gave him no comfort at all, because he knew for a fact that there were more vigilantes in Virginia City than he had bullets.

'W-w-what do you want?' he stammered.

The stranger favoured him with an icy smile that seemed only to complement his eyes. 'That's better. I had a feeling you'd be reasonable. What we want is Slade, sliced and diced. Simple as that. Oh, and don't even attempt to deny any knowledge of him.'

Plummer was aghast. 'Why?' was all he could manage this time.

'He's upset some people far more than you ever could, with your dwindling bunch of pathetic road agents. And I'll also allow that he's a very dangerous individual. I could kill every man here, including you, but I wouldn't want to tackle him on my lonesome unless I had a real good edge. So the deal is that when he finally gets here, you deliver him to us and then you get to stay alive to carry on selling your moose piss to these simple fools.'

Despite his very real alarm, Plummer was beginning to deeply resent the other man's complete self-assurance. It also occurred to him that someone in his employ had been talking more than was good for them. 'For Christ's sake,' he fumed silently. 'This is my place. I don't have to take this.'

Instinctively, he stabbed his right forefinger down hard on to the table, so that the single glass wobbled slightly. 'Now you listen to me, shit head,' he snarled. 'No one, but no one, threatens me in the Top Saloon. Savvy?'

The pain that suddenly overwhelmed him was all the more excruciating for being so totally unexpected. With terrible force, a blade had literally skewered his hand, effectively pinning it to the table. His assailant offered a mirthless grin as he inspected the bloody wreckage.

'That must really hurt. Happen it'll teach you a lesson about who you're dealing with.'

Plummer felt nauseous. Every nerve ending in his body seemed to be on fire. He wanted to scream out his agony, but with some of his regulars looking on with detached curiosity, that really wouldn't do. Instead, he glanced over at Hezekiah. The barkeeper, his eyes wide with surprise, had both hands under the counter and was *seemingly* undecided about what to do. His employer shook his head firmly and then moaned uncontrollably as the blade was roughly extracted from his mutilated extremity.

'You did right, Henry,' his persecutor opined, as he gratuitously wiped the honed steel clean on Plummer's jacket. 'Be kind of a shame if we *both* got cut in half by that shit-faced bartender's twelve gauge, wouldn't it?' He paused for a moment and then added, 'You think about what I said, now. We'll expect you to be in touch when Slade gets here.'

The saloon owner desperately tried to marshal his thoughts. 'But what if he just doesn't turn up?'

'Then you'll have had your card marked

for nothing,' his persecutor remarked with a dry chuckle. With that, he casually got to his feet, turned on his heels and strolled out, for all the world as though he'd just enjoyed a quiet drink with a friend. Not once had he even mentioned his name!

For long moments, Plummer remained seated: hunched over the table as his body soaked up the pain. His only concern was to get back to his room without falling over. Violence and bloodshed were common in his premises and it wouldn't do at all for the proprietor to be seen as weak. And there *was* one small consolation. His assailant might be uncommonly vicious, but if he had spent all day waiting to converse with him, then he couldn't be that intelligent. That fact might well help when it came time to take revenge. With this thought in mind, he finally turned to Hezekiah and this time mouthed two words, 'Bar towel.'

To give him his due, the bartender well knew what to do in such circumstances. He actually brought two towels:

one to wrap around the injury and one to mop up the pool of blood on the table. Unfortunately, his opening remarks demonstrated a complete lack of sympathy for his boss's plight.

'Hot dang. I ain't never seen speed like that. That cutting tool came from nowhere. A nasty evil cuss like him is definitely someone to ride wide of. Don't you think? Huh? Boss?'

Plummer gritted his teeth and wrapped the grubby towel around his hand. He could sense many eyes upon him and knew that few of them would be benign.

'Get me on my feet,' he snapped. 'And then get back behind the bar. Business as usual, you hear?'

'Sure, sure, boss,' Hezekiah muttered blandly, as he hooked an arm under his employer's left armpit and heaved. Secretly, he was really quite enjoying the other's distress.

Plummer muffled a groan, took a deep breath and walked stiffly over to the rear of the saloon. Finally reaching the sanctuary of his room, he abruptly turned and bellowed out, 'Next round's on the house, boys!' Then, to the sound of raucous cheering, he stumbled across the threshold, slammed the door shut and promptly threw up over his boots.

* * *

Completely unaware of the unhealthy interest being shown in him in Virginia City, Slade had covered a lot of ground before nightfall. Having earlier heard a deal of sustained gunfire to the southeast, he had then passed the night in a grove of pines without benefit of a cooking fire and with his horse's reins tied to his left leg. No damned Sioux buck was going to run his animal off, and in truth a cold camp had been no hardship. The weather was warm and he possessed a plentiful supply of beef jerky and pemmican.

Before drifting off to sleep he had pondered on the likely cause of the shooting. In all probability it had been the three young southerners, which in a way was a shame. A shame because they had maybe died needlessly at the hands of yet another war party, and a shame because they had turned down his offer. He could doubtless have made good use of some proficient shootists in the mining camp. The need for more men was one of the reasons that he had allowed himself to be detained at Fort Phil Kearny in the first place, but that wasn't going to happen again. He'd had a bellyful of the God damned US Army's *hospitality!* And besides, if he didn't get to Virginia City soon, that pus weasel Plummer would be sending out a search party.

With the arrival of first light, the big man had washed down a mouthful of the delicious pemmican with canteen water and then cautiously resumed his journey. He knew that there was another of Carrington's partially constructed forts somewhere up ahead on the Bighorn River, but not its exact location. And in any case, it was impossible to predict the whereabouts of any patrols that may have been sent out. If he happened across one, then he would just have to take his chances, because he sure as hell couldn't retrace his steps. And of course, as ill luck would have it, that was exactly what occurred.

Slade rounded a tight bend on the trail and there before him, large as life in the middle distance, was an army detail. Although prepared for such an event, he still cursed to himself, 'Not more of the poxy cockchafers,' whilst outwardly displaying great delight. 'I can't tell you how glad I am to see you fellas,' he hollered over to them, all the while waving enthusiastically.

The mounted patrol comprised five very nervous enlisted men, led by a young 'shavetail' who had to have been barely out of West Point. He duly signalled his men to halt and then carefully scrutinized the approaching white man. Normally, such an inexperienced officer would have been bolstered by a veteran non-com, but Carrington's force was badly over-stretched. Although immensely relieved that they weren't encountering redskins, the officer was perplexed as to how the rather menacing-looking individual came to be on the trail in the first place. With the stranger reining in before him, he put the question in what he hoped was a suitably authoritarian tone.

'What brings a civilian north on the Bozeman Trail, when I know for a fact that it's been closed by order of Colonel Carrington?'

Slade bared a set of discoloured teeth, in what he hoped was a welcoming smile. 'You're not wrong there, lieutenant. No siree, not wrong at all. Only the thing is, I ain't really a fully fledged civilian, on account of I work for Jim Bridger. I'm on my way to Fort CF Smith with a message from the colonel.'

Such news warmed the young officer's heart. So much so that he didn't even enquire whether said message was written or verbal. He just knew that it gave him a good excuse to curtail the patrol and return to safety.

'Well, I and my men are attached to Fort Smith,' he announced somewhat grandly. 'So I believe it is my plain duty to escort you back there.'

His men obviously agreed with him, because there were relieved smiles all round and the stranger was suddenly very welcome indeed.

'Come and join me at the head of the column and give me news of Phil Kearny, Mister,' the lieutenant added expectantly.

By *column*, he of course meant the five men, but the civilian quelled a sneer and instead responded with, 'The name's Slade, and I'd be right happy to, *sir*.'

More than satisfied, the young officer urged his horse around and the enlisted men followed suit. They set off at a walk, so as to allow the 'scout' to catch up. As Slade moved up behind them, a grim set came over his hard features. Simultaneously, he drew and cocked his revolver and pulled the hunting knife from its sheath.

The soldier nearest him on the right half-turned in surprise at the distinctive metallic sound, but sadly he was far too slow to affect the outcome. At almost point-blank range, Slade fired into the side of the man's head. The muzzle flash burnt both hair and flesh, but his victim was already past caring. As the corpse toppled sideways out of the saddle, Slade leaned forward and viciously thrust his blade deep into the right side of the other rearmost rider. An awful scream erupted from the bluecoat's lips, and suddenly chaos reigned.

The remaining four soldiers couldn't initially comprehend that they were under attack from one of their own. It had to be an Indian war party. As they milled around frantically searching for the enemy, Bridger's 'scout' dragged his knife from sucking flesh and ploughed directly into them. Again cocking and firing, he sent a ball straight into the chest of another luckless individual. Only then did the horrified lieutenant finally realize what was really happening — but by then it was too late.

Their attacker well knew how to keep

people off guard by utilizing confusion and fear. Howling like a demented berserker, he viciously spurred his animal forward again. This time they literally slammed into another horse and rider, sending them crashing to the ground.

Of the two men still left untouched, it was the private who tried to fight back. Desperately, he attempted to level his long and unwieldy Springfield. Facing the wrong direction to easily draw a bead with his revolver, Slade chose to holster it and launched himself bodily from the saddle. His massive frame collided with the struggling soldier and together they plummeted on to the rock-hard trail. As planned, his victim hit first and then had Slade's great weight land on top of him, effectively crushing him insensible.

Temporarily ignoring his powerless victim, the murderous predator next leapt up and rushed at the soldier who had gone down with his animal. Swaying on his hands and knees, that hapless individual never even saw the knife as it came from above and cleanly sliced through his jugular. Leaving him to bleed out, his killer finally turned his attention to the leader of the doomed patrol.

It was the second lieutenant's first action and it hadn't been anything like he'd imagined. For a start, his men had been comprehensively slaughtered by a fellow white man, which made absolutely no sense. And now, that terrifying apparition was coming directly for him. Instead of drawing his service revolver from its flap holster and charging the big bastard, the young officer simply panicked. Brutally yanking at the bit, he dug his heels into his horse's flanks and rode to safety. Or at least that's what he fervently prayed for.

His Spencer was still in its scabbard, so Slade drew his revolver and calmly and deliberately took aim with a two-handed grip. Drawing in a deep breath, he held it and fired. The heavy ball struck the fleeing lieutenant squarely between the shoulder blades, throwing him forward and conveniently delivering him under the pounding hoofs of his own mount. That animal finally got clear of its shattered, bloodstained owner and galloped away.

After savouring a brief moment of professional satisfaction, Slade rapidly glanced around to see who was left alive. The man who had broken his fall was obviously next. Still winded and frantically trying to suck air into his lungs, the enlisted man must have known that his plight was hopeless, because his eyes were like those of a terrified animal. Watching the huge executioner loom over him, he pathetically shook his head. Slade coldly surveyed him for a moment and then discharged yet another chamber, directly between his prey's eyes.

That death left only the soldier who had been stabbed in the back. He lay slumped over the withers of his animal, his uniform jacket sodden with blood. Slade cautiously approached him, gun at the ready, until he realized there was no cause for concern. Glassy, lifeless eyes stared back at him until he casually reached up and dragged the cadaver from the saddle.

Having single-handedly massacred the entire patrol, the big renegade pondered his next move whilst laboriously reloading his cap 'n ball revolver. He had two main priorities: to come out with a profit, and to lay the blame on someone else. The former was easy to achieve. After searching the surrounding terrain for any sign of trouble, he contentedly emptied the pockets of all the enlisted men. His haul included a gratifying number of silver dollars, plus a useful supply of paper cartridges and percussion caps. The lead balls in the cartridges were of too large a calibre for his weapons, but he decided to discard those later, when he was well clear of the area. It would be worth making that effort to obtain a fresh supply of gunpowder.

By now his bloodlust had cooled, and Slade was beginning to feel the onset of an unaccustomed uneasiness. Standing in silence, surrounded by the blood-soaked bodies of his own race, he decided that it was definitely time to be on his way. But first there was his latter priority to achieve. If his victims were discovered by their comrades, those men needed to think that Indians were to blame.

Lips curled with distaste, he seized hold of a full head of hair on the nearest corpse and began to slice through the scalp. After repeating that repugnant action twice more and with his hands greasy with blood, he had more than had enough.

'How the hell can anybody enjoy doing this?' he muttered. Dragging a jacket off one of his victims, he rolled the scalps up in it and then thrust the bundle in a saddle-bag. Then he wiped his hands on the long grass and glanced wistfully over at the distant figure of the prone lieutenant. He well knew that his take might be even better from an officer, but with the cessation of violence a dreadful tiredness was beginning to overcome him, and he was also nervous about just who all that shooting might attract. So, gratefully mounting his powerful horse, he moved off up the trail without a backward glance.

7

'It just don't make sense, you disarming all of us out here,' Charlie complained for maybe the third time that day. 'What if we get jumped by another bunch of hostiles?'

Sergeant Rudabauer was well used to the bellyaching of young recruits and so completely ignored him, but after a lifetime in the wild regions, Bridger never had adjusted to the continuous company of his fellow man.

'For Christ's sake,' he exclaimed. 'Don't you young fellas ever know when to . . . ?' The old scout's mouth shut like a trap, as he abruptly reined his horse to a stop. Silently, he gazed off into the distance, oblivious to the tobacco juice that was seeping through his lips and down his bristly chin. His companions sat their animals and observed him curiously. There was a strange faraway look to his eyes, which made them all vaguely uncomfortable. It was as though he had sensed something of great import that had completely eluded them.

Finally, Rudabauer could take it no longer. After all, he was supposed to be at least nominally in charge. 'What is it, Jim?' he softly enquired, masking his impatience. 'What have you seen, or heard, or . . . anything?'

For a long moment, Bridger remained silent. Then he finally settled his eyes on the other man. 'Up ahead. Something ain't right.' A pause, then, 'Better hand over their shooting irons. They just might could need them.'

As the three young men gratefully received and readied their weapons, the former mountain man urged his horse forward, all the while sniffing the air like some sort of wild creature. 'I reckon whatever it is, is round that tight bend up ahead. I'm going to take a look see.'

Rudabauer regarded him dubiously. 'You right sure you want to do that?'

The army scout shrugged. 'It's what I

get paid to do. And so do you. So if all hell breaks loose, I'd appreciate a little help.' He offered a wry smile. 'I'm sure you'll know *hell* if you hear it.' With that, he moved off alone to discover just what his sixth sense had alerted him to.

Waylan was mystified. 'How can he know something's wrong, when there's nothing to see?'

The sergeant shook his head. 'Search me. I'm a soldier and a damn good one, but I got my service in back east, shooting at people like you.'

As Bridger disappeared from sight, the four men waited anxiously for any sign that something was amiss. Long minutes passed without any disclosure, until finally Rudabauer had again had enough. 'Shit in a bucket! I've had my fill of this waiting. Are you fellas with me?'

'Are you asking or telling?' Charlie demanded, fingering his Henry and prickly as ever.

'Asking,' the sergeant reluctantly responded and was presently gratified to discover that all three southerners were advancing along the trail with him.

What they discovered was both a relief *and* a waking nightmare. There wasn't an Indian in sight, but the old scout was kneeling on the ground, literally surrounded by blue-clad corpses. As the four men approached, he favoured them with a quick glance, before painfully getting to his feet. Massaging his bad hip, he slowly moved from body to body, occasionally bending down to check on something.

On reaching the terrible scene, Rudabauer gazed around in utter dismay. His pulse was racing and his forehead felt suddenly clammy. 'Jesus, but those savages make a mess!' he bitterly exclaimed.

Bridger suddenly stared at the unhappy non-com. 'You ever known Indians to steal cash money off of a white man?'

The sergeant shrugged. 'I ain't been out here long enough to rightly know what they do.'

'Well, take it from me; it weren't any Sioux or Cheyenne that did all this. It was whites trying to make it look like Indians, only they spoilt it by getting greedy.'

Taylor, always quiet and serious, had studied the soldiers carefully. 'But what about the scalping?'

'That's nothing,' Bridger retorted scornfully. 'And it's the other thing that's not right about all this. They look too damn good! If it had been Indians, these boys would be sliced up, disembowelled and biting on their own peckers.'

Before anyone could respond, Waylan's sharp eyes detected movement. 'I'm sure that fellow over yonder just twitched some,' he announced, wheeling his mount around and making straight for the young officer. What he found did little to lighten the overall mood.

The second lieutenant had quite obviously been shot in the back, but looking at his cuts, bruises and distorted limbs that appeared to be the least of his worries.

'Water,' he croaked.

As the others joined him, Waylan

produced a canteen. Sadly, more liquid was spilt than swallowed, but Bridger was in no mood to pussyfoot around. 'Who did this to you?' he barked out.

Pain-wracked eyes attempted to focus on him. The young officer's breathing was coming in short gasps. He obviously didn't have long.

The grizzled scout tried again. 'Who was it killed you?' Seizing Waylan's canteen, he callously tipped water over the dying man's face. The sudden shock got a response of sorts.

'Never . . . seen . . . nothing . . . like . . . him.'

'Who?' Bridger bellowed.

'S . . . Slade.' That one word was the last anyone would get out of the lieutenant, because his breath abruptly gave out. But it was enough.

'God damn it all to hell,' Rudabauer exclaimed. 'That murdering varmint's worse than I thought by far.' He glanced at the three southerners. Their genuine shock was plain to see, but that couldn't alter the situation. Rapidly coming to a decision, he remarked, 'Right, we're taking this body to Fort Smith and reporting in. If they've got such a thing, you three fellas can cool your heels in the guardhouse for a spell, while Bridger and me go after that cockchafer.'

The southerners' reaction to that announcement was instantaneous. Simultaneously, all three of them swung their rifles over to cover their two captors.

'You're kind of forgetting something,' Waylan remarked. 'You've just rearmed us and there ain't no way we're being locked in any Union stockade.'

Rudabauer had his revolver vaguely pointing in their direction, but he recognized that they had him outgunned. And yet strangely, he wasn't for backing down. 'You men are my prisoners,' he stubbornly informed them. 'The only way that's gonna change, is if you pull those triggers. Only thing is, if you do then you'll be no different to your buddy, Slade.'

Waylan spoke for all of them when he answered that. 'We ain't nothing like

Slade and he ain't our friend. I'll allow he did save my life, but I think he had a certain reason for that and in any case it can't excuse what he's done here. God knows we've got reason enough to hate you Yankees, but this just wasn't right.'

The sergeant was, if nothing else, a pragmatist. 'So what have you got in mind?'

Waylan glanced meaningfully at his friends and they nodded assent. 'You two fellas do what you have to do at the fort. Slade's making for Virginia City and so are we and I reckon this bloodbath confirms that it's him alone that you want for Hoffman's murder. We'll join up with you after the fort and help you catch him, but whatever occurs we're *not* going back to stand trial in front of Carrington. We just want to clear our names and be left in peace. Deal?'

Rudabauer glanced over at Bridger, who merely shrugged. 'It's your call. I'm just along to help make it happen.'

The soldier grunted. 'A lot of help

you are.' Turning back to the others, he nodded. 'Deal. How will we find you once we're clear of the fort?'

Waylan chuckled. 'Oh, that's easy. Just whistle Dixie and we'll find you.'

Charlie motioned towards the murdered detail's grazing horses. 'Me riding double will slow us all down, so I'll help myself to one of those animals. Yeah?'

Rudabauer nodded. 'I guess the army can spare one.'

Taylor was puzzled. 'Just why are you taking this body in and leaving the rest?'

'Huh,' the other man exclaimed. 'For the same reason I've been butting up against you lot. Unlike the others, this poor child was an officer and the post commander will likely report favourably on me for bringing his body in before carrion birds and the like get at it. I aim to make sergeant-major one day, and such things help.'

★ ★ ★

Sheer bad luck alone can often be enough to bring a man down, and Wendell Storey had unwittingly already had a sizeable dose of it. Dispirited at not having encountered a single living soul on the Bozeman Trail, he had decided to steal a little shuteye in one of the many groves of trees that bordered it. As a direct consequence, the burly bruiser had missed spotting, by only a few minutes, the very individual that his boss was so desperate to see, and in doing so had extended his own journey quite considerably. As Slade's still bloodstained figure had ridden past, Plummer's enforcer dozed in blissful ignorance.

So it was that much later that day, Storey caught his first glimpse of Fort CF Smith. Like its counterpart further down the trail, it was currently little more than a collection of tents, with mountain howitzers forming the main deterrent. Even so, it represented authority and therefore made him nervous. As he gazed down on the construction activity from a low rise to the north, his slow mind mulled over what to do. It took long moments, but he finally decided that he had no choice. The sole way to discover why all traffic on the trail had ceased, was to go and ask those who would know. Only then could he legitimately turn around and return to Virginia City.

Sighing with resignation, Storey urged his animal off to the left and down to the fort. Typically, after struggling with the awkward beast for miles, his horse now smelt fresh water and voluntarily picked up speed. The Bighorn River, literally flowing next to the fort, glistened in the glorious sunshine, but such magnificent scenery was completely lost on the new arrival. He had spotted an officer taking his ease, smoking a cigar in front of a tent and decided to make for him. Only men of importance could lounge around whilst others worked, he reasoned. Such a man would surely know the situation on the Bozeman.

Uneasily, Storey viciously urged his horse on to army property, away from the sparkling water that it naturally desired. Sentries armed with rifles watched him closely. He didn't look anything like an Indian, but that didn't seem to make any difference. For some reason they appeared to be skittish and on edge. Unfamiliar with military etiquette, the civilian rode straight past the expectant sergeant of the guard and fetched up directly before the cigar-smoking captain. Storey barely noticed the incessant hammering and sawing as he tried to formulate some words.

'Hey there, general,' was his best stab at a greeting.

The moustachioed officer gazed up at him with mild amusement, taking in the massive Colt Dragoon tucked in his belt, but otherwise offering no response.

Doggedly, Storey tried again. 'Top Saloon. Virginia City.'

'What of it?' came the curt reply.

'My boss wants to know why his whiskey ain't arriving.'

As realization dawned on the soldier, a sly smile spread across his lean features. It had been some considerable time since he'd had anything to chuckle at. 'That's probably because the enlisted men took it upon themselves to drink it all!' he quickly responded.

Storey's intelligence was strictly limited and he fell for that hook, line and sinker. A strangled cry of, 'Whaat?' was all he could muster.

The captain guffawed loudly, before deciding that the pitiful oaf really wasn't worth any more effort. 'Just funning, mister. Just funning.' He then proceeded to explain, in very simple language, just what Colonel Carrington had done and why.

'Oh shit!' Storey exclaimed. 'So nothing and nobody's getting through, huh?'

The captain was by this time thoroughly bored with the conversation and so merely nodded. The unhappy civilian groaned with dismay. 'So I've got another long ride on this ornery critter and only bad news to tell at the end of it. My boss's gonna be mighty sore when he hears of this. It ain't just about the joy juice. He was really set on seeing his new hired hand as well.'

'Time to get rid of this moron,' the soldier finally decided. He said, 'A drink or three at the sutler's might ease the pain before you go. Tell him I sent you.' With that, he abruptly turned away to finish his cigar in peace. Why he suddenly asked a parting question, he would probably never know. Perhaps it was just honest curiosity from an officer who prided himself on knowing everything that occurred in his command. 'What do they call this hired hand anyway? Just in case he should turn up in the future.'

Storey should have known better, but his mind was already on the jug with his moniker on it. And who was to say, that if he found that the 'rot gut' was to his taste, he might not just end up passing the night at Fort CF Smith? The name already had a good ring to it, even if he had no idea what the hell CF meant. Hopelessly pre-occupied, he uttered just one word: 'Slade.'

Captain Connor had long since forgotten his uninspiring conversation with Wendell Storey. He had two particularly serious problems on his mind. Both the hay-cutting detail and the Bozeman patrol were late back. Especially the patrol, which was long overdue. So when the sergeant of the guard reported that riders were approaching from the south-east, Conner rushed expectantly for the perimeter. Unfortunately, what he saw did nothing to lessen his anxiety. Where there should have been at least six horsemen, there were only two, leading a number of riderless animals. Then came the heart-stopping moment when he realized that there was a body slung over a trailing horse. That was swiftly displaced by a flash of recognition.

'Isn't that Mister Bridger in the lead?' he asked the sergeant.

'I reckon so, sir. And I recognize the man with him. Sergeant Rudabauer, assigned to Fort Phil Kearny.'

'I wonder what brings them here?' Conner mused. 'I just hope to God that that cadaver isn't one of ours.' Thankfully, he didn't have long to wait, but what the new arrivals had to both show and tell him would bring no succour.

Of the two visitors reined in before him, it was the scout who initially 'bit the bullet' and reported the grim tidings. 'There ain't no easy way to say it. This here's some of what's left of your patrol, Captain.'

Leaving his companion to supply the grisly details, Bridger gingerly dismounted. Groaning at the sudden spasm of pain in his right hip, he remarked to the crowd of onlookers that had gathered, 'I'm getting too old for all of this.' Unsurprisingly, no one even heard him. To a man, they were all listening with rapt attention to Rudabauer's graphic description of events.

The captain was incredulous. 'One white man did all that?'

'That's what the lieutenant said, just before he died, sir.'

Connor suddenly became aware of all the gawkers surrounding him. Angrily, he ordered, 'You men, return to your duties, immediately. Sergeant, lead the body over to the surgeon's tent. He can arrange a burial. And then organize a detail to ride out and recover the other bodies.'

Once everyone had departed, the harassed officer was left alone with the newcomers. 'You've done well, Sergeant Rudabauer. I will make mention of it in my next report to the colonel.'

Rudabauer's eyes momentarily caught Bridger's as he replied, 'Why thank you, sir. That'd be much appreciated.'

'If only we knew the identity of this crazed assassin.'

It was Bridger who answered. 'Slade ain't crazed, Captain. Merely very dangerous.'

The officer's eyes widened in disbelief. 'Slade! I had some cretin asking about just such a man, barely one hour ago.'

Five men stood a short distance from the sutler's capacious tent. In addition to the captain and the new arrivals, there were two enlisted men. One of these carried a set of iron manacles.

'Can you recall if he was toting a side-arm, Captain?' Bridger enquired softly.

'Of course I did,' replied the other man with a hint of indignation. 'He had a big old horse pistol stuffed down his pants.'

The old scout still wasn't finished, but he was aware that he was encroaching on another man's territory. 'Don't like to mention it after what's happened, Captain, but we need this man alive. Colonel Carrington will want to see Slade dangling from a rope and anything this ass boil can tell us about the situation in Virginia City will be useful, because that's where we're likely to catch up with him.'

Connor was out for blood, but he was also a conscientious officer who could see the sense in such advice.

'Very well, Mister Bridger. Since he knows me, I will go in and engage him in conversation. I will endeavour to grab his revolver and leave the rest to you and Rudabauer.'

Without more ado, the tall officer strode over to the tent and ducked under its open flap. The interior was just as he had expected. The far end was dominated by a long, substantial trestle table, behind which stood the sutler. A big, heavyset individual, his beady eyes were alert to everything that happened in his domain. Around the sides of the enclosed space were stacked barrels and sacks containing every conceivable commodity, including tobacco, coffee, sugar and flour. The various aromas mingled to produce a smell that was not at all unpleasant and certainly a welcome change from the military's ever-present odour of sweat.

Because all of the enlisted men were on either fatigue or guard duties, the tent's only other occupant was Wendell Storey. The sutler glanced over with surprise at the new arrival. It was not often that the captain frequented his establishment. Before the merchant could offer any comment, Connor brusquely shook his head in warning and then concentrated all his attention on his prey.

Having already sunk an astonishing quantity of cheap 'bug juice', the burly thug had no inkling of the officer's presence until that man slapped him 'playfully' on his back. As Storey turned in bleary surprise, Connor remarked, 'I hope you're being well looked after. You're a man of great interest to me.'

With his mind fogged by whiskey, Storey's bloodshot eyes widened and he raised his arms to embrace his new friend. As he did so, Connor seized the Colt Dragoon and roughly dragged it out from behind a foul-smelling waistband. Before his prisoner could even react, there followed a rush of bodies as the other four men entered the tent. More by animal instinct than logical thought, Storey suddenly recognized that he was under threat. Growling incoherently, he attempted to rise from the wooden stool that had been supporting his great weight.

Rudabauer swiftly came up behind him. Knowing full well that the frame of his Colt Army revolver could not absorb too much rough usage, he had borrowed a wooden mallet from one of the stockade's workers. With great relish, he now whacked his victim over the side of the head with it. Such a blow would have felled most normal men, but in Storey's case it merely sent him to his knees.

'What the hell's occurring here, Captain?' roared the sutler.

'You keep out of this, Mister Peabody,' the soldier retorted. 'It's army business and you're on army property. You'd do well to remember that!' Turning to the two enlisted men, he barked out, 'Get those irons on him before he recovers.'

The men hastened to comply, and by the time Storey's limited wits had returned, he was secured both hand and foot. His captors then heaved him back on the stool and Connor began to fire questions at him.

'What is your connection with the man Slade? Who does he work for? Why are you really here?' He suddenly stopped and waited eagerly for a reply. Any kind of reply. What he actually got was a rude shock.

The big brute peered at him through pain-wracked eyes and then abruptly spat a great gobbet of phlegm directly into his interrogator's face. The officer recoiled with shock, but swiftly recovered. With the slimy yellow matter still clinging to him, he landed a stinging smack on the other man's pasty features.

'I'll slap you red if you don't answer my questions!' he bellowed angrily.

'Haw, haw, haw,' responded Storey. It might have been the strong liquor talking, but he didn't appear in the least bit concerned at the captain's threat. 'It'll take more than a pussy like you to make me talk. My old pa used to bounce me off the walls before the sun was even up.'

Connor grabbed an old piece of sacking to wipe his face and give him time to think. Despite being in charge of a fort and its entire garrison, he had no real idea of what to do next. After all, he was a soldier, not a medieval torturer. Conveniently, Jim Bridger had no such scruples.

'Hold his right hand flat on the table,' he instructed. 'I'll make the varmint talk.'

The enlisted men turned to their commander who, after a moment's contemplation, gave a curt nod. One of the privates yanked hard on a manacle and then lowered his whole weight on to Storey's right arm, so that that individual's hand was trapped against the rough planking. His mug of whiskey toppled over, spilling its contents, but that was suddenly the least of his troubles.

Bridger ambled around to the other side of the table, forcing the sutler to reluctantly give ground. The old scout looked directly into his captive's eyes.

'You try spitting in my face an' I'll stitch your lips together with a horse needle.'

The words came out like chips of ice and left Storey in no doubt that he was up against someone entirely different. What he witnessed next did nothing to ease his sudden fear. Bridger produced an obviously well honed knife, followed by a chill smile.

'I learnt me this trick from an Arikara Indian many years ago, before the smallpox laid 'em all low. Unless you really want me to show you it, you'd better answer the captain's questions, pronto!'

Storey retained enough Dutch courage to display his contempt. 'Go suck on a prickly pear, you old bastard!'

Bridger nodded slowly, as though he had fully expected such a response. 'Fair enough. I guess, looking at that scar on your cheek, you're no stranger to knives, but this might come as a surprise. So, now, spread your fingers.'

'Whaat?'

'Spread 'em or lose 'em, mister!'

With obvious reluctance, the prisoner extended his grubby digits until the table was visible between them. The knifepoint abruptly pricked the wood between forefinger and thumb and then went on to methodically touch down between the others. As its course was reversed, it picked up speed.

'What the hell are you about?' Storey howled. Suddenly stone-cold sober, his belligerence was dissipating rapidly.

Bridger froze in mid-stroke and favoured his victim with a feral grin. 'Well, I'll tell you, big man. The longer you hold out, the faster I go. But the thing is, I ain't as nimble as I used to be and my eyesight could be better. Sooner or later, I'm gonna miss and cut you up real bad.'

'You're mad!'

'It's been said,' Bridger answered laconically, returning to his task with greater gusto. As the blade stabbed down in sequence between his fingers with bewildering and terrifying speed,

Storey attempted to pull away, but that had two consequences. The soldier applied even more weight to his arm *and* Bridger missed. As the knifepoint pierced his middle finger to the bone, the hapless thug screamed with pain. With his life-blood flowing over the trestle table and mingling with whiskey from the over-turned mug, he stared in horror at his tormentor. Perhaps he was simply in shock, but whatever the reason he still didn't appear ready to talk.

Carrington's scout paused momen-tarily to remark, 'Now look what you've made me do,' before immediately resum-ing his frightening 'game'. His audience looked on almost mesmerized, as the pace picked up even more. Then the edge of the blade sliced through soft flesh at the base of his victim's little finger and all resistance ended.

'I'll talk,' Storey screamed, sweat pour-ing from his face. His relief, as the knife froze in mid-air, was almost pathetic to behold. 'I don't know why you want him,' he blurted out. 'But Slade's got a job to go to in Virginia City. Henry Plummer needs him to kill a few people. It's what he's good at.'

'Who's Plummer?' Connor snapped.

'My boss. He owns the Top Saloon, but he also runs a gang of road agents and claim jumpers. There ain't no law of any kind in Virginia City, but the thing is, some of the big operators led by a man name of Stuart are fighting back to take control, and Plummer needs help.'

'This big operator. Is Stuart his first or last name?'

'How the hell should I know?' whined Storey. 'He wouldn't piss on the likes of me if I was on fire!'

'And what brings you here?'

'Slade's overdue. Plummer sent me looking, that's all. Honest, I ain't done nothing wrong.'

The captain snorted. 'Looking at you, I reckon you've done plenty wrong in your time.' Nevertheless, it was obvious that he was satisfied.

With alarming deftness, Jim Bridger

changed his grip on the knife, so that its razor-sharp point was abruptly drawing blood under Storey's chin. A gap-toothed grin spread across his grizzled features.

'Now that wasn't so difficult, was it?'

8

The following afternoon found Slade concealed behind a boulder, on the crest of a rocky rise, well outside Virginia City's limits. His journey through the elevated Bozeman Pass had been uneventful but gruelling. Having slaked his thirst in the Flathead River, he was now eager for a *proper* drink, a bathhouse and a whore. In that order. And yet only a fool would blunder into a strange town without taking the time to check it out. Consequently, he was carefully scrutinizing the place though a small drawtube spyglass. Having taken a shine to it, he had stolen the glass some years earlier from a railroad surveyor in Nebraska Territory. It was worn and battered, but nothing like as much as the surveyor had been by the time that Slade was finished with him. It still made him smirk to think of the incident.

To his cynical eye, Virginia City appeared pretty much how all mining boomtowns looked. Even during the day, when most of the men might be expected to be at the nearby diggings, the mud-churned streets were crowded. Amongst a haphazard mixture of grubby tents and cabins, people were doing business of every sort. Animals, clothes, mining tools and women were all for sale. And then there were the more substantial buildings, constructed by those who had got there first and made it big, or by shady businessmen intending to leech off the inhabitants. Slade smiled to himself, as he reflected on the fact that Henry Plummer was one of the most efficient leeches that he had so far encountered.

For long minutes, the massive gun thug patiently panned his spyglass over the camp and its surroundings, until finally he spotted something that just didn't look right. A lone figure lingered amongst a small clutch of trees, off to the side of the trail into town. He was obviously a lookout, bought and paid for and set to watch for someone's arrival. The question was, *who* was paying him?

And Slade didn't like unanswered questions. Lingering possibilities put him on edge and affected his work. Therefore he would have to visit with this lonely soul and perhaps end his life. With his horse already safely tethered, he contracted the glass and commenced a laborious detour on foot. Because this entailed a deal of unwelcome exertion, his mood was dark and his mind occupied by bloody thoughts.

★   ★   ★

Jason Matlock was plagued by two competing emotions: boredom and gnawing hunger. He had been confined to the diminutive copse since first light, and even though the sun was long past its zenith, no one had thought to bring him any hot food. Apparently a canteen of water and some beef jerky were to be his only sustenance for the remainder of the day.

His instructions were to keep watch on the start (or was it the end?) of the Bozeman Trail until nightfall, for anyone at all that might arrive. Since it was obvious, to anybody with half a brain, that the trail had been closed for many a day, there had unsurprisingly been nothing to report and nothing to do. Initially, the giddy excitement of being picked for the task had kept him going, but that had long since passed.

'God dammit,' he exclaimed under his breath. 'What I wouldn't give for a plate of steak and beans.'

The sudden sharp pain in the side of his neck was excruciating, but his opportunity to cry out was extinguished by a horny palm clamped over his mouth. Instinctively, his right hand dropped to his holstered Colt, but that was definitely a bad move. Simultaneously, the pain increased and a low voice snarled, 'Don't! Your hand touches that iron, it'll be the last thing you do. Savvy?'

Jason froze, his extremity barely an inch from the revolver butt. He could feel blood trickling down into his shirt collar. 'Sweet Jesus, mister. I ain't no threat to you.' The muffled statement was concluded with an anguished croak.

Slade offered a mirthless chuckle. 'You got that plumb right, sonny. Question is, just what brings you out here? It sure ain't the company.' Even as he spoke, the ruffian relaxed his left hand slightly, but at the same time increased his pressure on the knife, increasing the flow of blood and eliciting a low moan from the young man.

'I'm supposed to watch out for some big gun hand, name of Slade. Either alone or with a gang.'

The 'big gun hand' grunted non-committedly. The answer to his next question would determine whether Jason lived or died. 'And just who might you be working for?'

There was a moment's silence, as shocked realization dawned. 'God almighty! You're him, ain't you? The man they're waiting on. It's said you've kilt nigh on *twenty* men.'

'Are you working for Henry Plummer?' Slade persisted.

'The hell I am,' Jason exclaimed, his youthful belligerence momentarily overcoming the pain. 'He's one of them murdering, claim-jumping Innocents, using the Top Saloon as cover.'

'Seems like there's nothing more to be said,' Slade remarked almost conversationally, as he abruptly sliced the blade deep into Jason's exposed throat. He then held on tightly, as his dying victim jerked and twitched through his death throes. Only when all movement had ceased, did he finally lower the silent, blood-soaked body to the ground. A fair amount of the greasy fluid had spread to his own clothes, which by now resembled the property of a slaughter man. A more fastidious individual would have been revolted, but to Slade it just came with the job.

'Oh, and *twenty* don't even come close, young fella.'

* * *

'Dead! What the hell do you mean, he's dead? All he was doing was sitting around in a bunch of trees.' The speaker was a strongly built individual in his forties. He had close-cropped hair and sported a neatly trimmed beard. Any man in Virginia City who had time and money to spend on his appearance had to be a man of substance. Granville Stuart was just such a man.

'Some son of a bitch sawed through his throat from ear to ear, real unfriendly like,' responded Bill 'the beast' Bunton. 'Whoever did it, knew what they were about. It was a quality piece of work, leaving no chance of survival. It's rumoured that that pus weasel Plummer is a fair hand with a blade, but after what I did to his, I really don't reckon it was him.'

The two men were sitting in Stuart's office, which formed part of a substantial building situated across the dirt thoroughfare from the Top Saloon. The large upstairs room was lit solely by three flickering candles. He had taken against oil lamps, ever since his younger

141

brother had been horribly burned to death when one containing kerosene had been thrown at him. This had occurred during a dispute involving, amongst others, a notorious gun thug by the name of Slade.

Stuart was a prospector who had got in early and made it big. He was also the driving force behind the vigilante movement that bore his name. The camp's stakeholders were no longer prepared to tolerate lawlessness and daylight robbery, but unfortunately the only way to control it was to use similarly brutal methods. Hence the menacing presence of Bill 'the beast' Bunton.

That man had not come by his colourful nickname lightly. He had earned it with a series of increasingly brutal murders towards the end of the California Gold Rush, and then it had just kind of stuck. Since then, he had made it plain that he was not offended by its use.

Stuart glanced sharply at his enforcer. 'Well, someone did it and I want him found and brought to account. Jesus Christ, I promised Jason's pa that I'd look after the boy, and the best I can do now is send him back east in a box.'

Bunton was unimpressed. 'I suppose taking care of him meant leaving him out there all day without any food, huh? As a favour to his pa.' His cold eyes glinted dangerously as he spoke. Both men knew that he was testing his employer. Searching for weakness. Seeing just how far he could push. A man with his skills got used to being on the prod. Stuart knew all of that, and yet wasn't about to take any nonsense. Not while he held the purse strings.

'While you're on wages from me, you'll bridle that tongue, understand? Or we'll get to falling out and the *dinero* will stop.' He waited long moments until the other man favoured him with a barely perceptible nod, before finally continuing. 'I want more pitch torches lit and men out on the street watching the Top Saloon. I'd like to bring the whole place down around Plummer's ears, but the time's not right. There's something occurring. I can smell it and I want to know just what it is. So move!'

For a brief moment Bunton remained in his chair, coolly scrutinizing his employer. He was literally trying to decide whether to gut him like a fish or act on his orders. It was the prospect of a big payday that ultimately kept his knife in its sheath. After all, there was no all-fired hurry. Nodding slowly, he got to his feet and made for the door, but the hired killer couldn't resist one final jibe.

'If you want my advice, I wouldn't go wasting your gold flake on a pine box, boss. Send sweet young Jason back east in this heat and all they'll get is offal.' A sardonic smirk crossed the 'beast's' lean features, and then he was gone.

⋆   ⋆   ⋆

Henry Plummer felt a growing sense of uneasiness, the like of which he hadn't experienced in all his time in the mining camp. For one thing, his injured hand throbbed abominably, and then there was Wendell Storey. Or rather there wasn't, because the great oaf seemed to have disappeared without trace. To cap it all, someone had stationed a young gun hand in the trees on the outskirts of town, and for all Plummer knew he was still there. But to what end? He swore bitterly. The situation appeared to be getting away from him.

Darkness had fallen and the raucous sounds of alcohol-fuelled enjoyment grew louder. He knew that he should really be out in the saloon, seeing to business, but his heart just wasn't in it. Sighing gloomily, he decided to have a peaceful smoke instead. The atmosphere in his bedroom seemed suddenly oppressive. He needed to take in some night air. After extinguishing the sole kerosene lamp, he moved to the far end of the room and carefully eased back the two large bolts on the door that served as his private escape route.

Stepping out into the inky blackness at the rear of the Top Saloon, Plummer elected to light his roll-up while his night vision was still limited. Extracting a Lucifer from his pocket, he turned to ignite it on the rough timber. An instant before it could flare into life, he was abruptly seized in a bear-like grip that felt totally overwhelming. Then a hand closed over his mouth, leaving him no chance to react, and a vaguely familiar voice whispered into his ear.

'How's it hanging, Henry?'

Recognition came in a flash. As he was yanked backwards into his own premises and the hand over his mouth loosened slightly, he hissed, 'Hell's teeth, is that you, Slade?'

There was a dry chuckle. 'The very same. You're getting a mite careless in your old age, you dodgy bastard.' With that, the man that Plummer had been so desperately awaiting released his new employer.

No longer under restraint, that individual was able to relight the lamp and peer over at the massive apparition. 'Where are the others?' he enquired expectantly.

'What others? There ain't any others. Just me.'

Surprised, the saloon owner tried again. 'So what have you done with Wendell?'

'Who the hell's Wendell?'

Bewilderment was turning to annoyance. 'He works for me. I sent him to find you.'

'Uhuh. Well mayhap he got picked up by the army. Those soldier boys have closed the trail to all civilian traffic. Or he could even have been skinned alive by some of the Godless heathens they're supposed to be fighting. One thing's for sure, he ain't with me.'

Plummer snorted with annoyance and then took his first really good look at the nocturnal visitor. His eyes widened with surprise at the amount of blood on Slade's clothes. 'What in God's name have you been about?'

The other man grunted. 'You might say I took a *blood bath* back on the trail. And then there was that kid in the trees. He sure was a messy bleeder.'

Plummer began to feel queasy, but before he could comment, Slade had more to say. 'You know this place is being watched, don't you? The main street is lit up like the fourth of July. That's why I had to skulk around out back in the dark like some kind of felon. Are they the same fellas that took agin your shooting hand?'

Instinctively, Plummer protectively cradled his injured extremity. 'Nah. They'll be just foot soldiers. The man that did this to me was something special. I'll be expecting you to see to him.'

Slade's professional curiosity was aroused. 'Special how?'

Plummer grimaced at the memory. 'He took me apart in my own place without even breaking sweat, as though he did it every day. He was real lean, with the coldest eyes I've ever seen. *And* he knew of you. Seemed to rate you pretty high.'

'Bunton!'

Despite the heat, Plummer shivered. 'Bill the beast?'

A strange, distant look seemed to have crept into Slade's eyes, but his response was instantaneous. 'The very same. Seems to me you were lucky he didn't saw that hand clean off!'

Plummer suddenly recollected something. 'That kid. Did you really have to kill him? All it'll do is get Stuart even more riled.'

Slade glanced at him scornfully. 'He would have told them about me. This way they don't know for sure who did it, which gives us an edge. And believe me, with Bill Bunton in town you're gonna need one. He ain't too bright, but he's one mean son of a bitch. Hell, the thought of tangling with him has even taken my mind off of the whores you could have waiting for me.'

'Whores be damned,' his employer exclaimed somewhat unnecessarily. 'There's matters here need setting aright. I want to know what you're going to do about them. That's what I'm paying you for.'

'You ain't paid me doodly-squat yet,' Slade growled.

Plummer stared at him for a moment, before moving over to the massive iron safe situated next to his bed. Once unlocked, he heaved open the heavy door and extracted a leather purse, which he tossed over to his massive enforcer.

'There's fifty gold simoleons in there, and more to come when you've earned them. So I'll ask you again, what are your plans?'

Slade's fingers closed around the purse as he answered. 'Fair enough, but I ain't about to go off half cock. I need to know the lie of the land and exactly what I'm up against. But first I want hot food and to sleep the clock around. The Bozeman turned out to be a hard trail to travel and I'm no use to you dog tired and starving.'

Despite his eagerness, Henry Plummer could see the sense in all of that. 'Agreed, but we need to keep you hidden for a while. Even from those that work in the saloon. I reckon one of them's passing information on to Stuart and I've a fair idea who. I'll have food brought in as though it's for me and you can use my bed. Where's your horse?'

'Tethered in the rocks behind that low rise on the way in to town.'

'I'll bring it in to the livery myself.'

Slade suddenly favoured him with a wolfish grin. 'You're treating me real good, Henry. Pretty soon I'll have to see about repaying all this kindness!'

9

'I don't like towns,' declared Jim Bridger. 'The air in them stinks. Too many people, too little space.'

'Well, I guess that means you'll be watching our backs then,' Rudabauer responded. 'Because one way or another I reckon it ends here.'

Unknowingly, the five men had just dismounted on the same spot from which their murderous quarry had scrutinized the camp the previous afternoon. After leaving Fort CF Smith, the sergeant had indeed whistled 'Dixie' and, as agreed, the three southerners had voluntarily rejoined Colonel Carrington's diminutive pursuit party. From then on it had been a trouble-free ride through the Bozeman Pass, following in Slade's tracks. They arrived on the outskirts of Virginia City in the early evening.

It was unlikely that any of the

inhabitants would have any knowledge of their coming. They hadn't encountered so much as a single traveller, and Captain Connor had willingly agreed to assign a desperately unhappy Wendell Storey to the next hay-cutting detail . . . unarmed and under guard. 'Unpaid hard labour may well teach him the error of associating with a man like Slade,' the officer had grimly remarked. 'And with any luck he might even get himself killed by the Cheyenne!'

Waylan had obviously been thinking things over. 'The way I see it, we don't want to enter a strange town at night. With no law, the place could be a real snake pit. We should cold camp up here and move in at first light.'

The others all concurred and so four of them carefully backed away from the vantage point. Bridger chose to remain and do what he did best: observe. Settling down on the ground with his spyglass, he remarked, 'You fellas divvy up the vittles. I'll maybe join you when the light's gone.'

As it happened, darkness had fallen completely by the time the old scout rejoined them, and he had a tale to tell. 'Seems like this Virginia City's got more than just prospecting and trading going on. I spotted the Top Saloon that we teased out of Wendell. It's lit up by pitch torches, with fellas outside watching it that by rights you'd expect would be inside swilling whiskey. And that ain't the least of it. Just before the light went, I recognized one of the men down there: Bill Bunton, sometimes known as the Beast. A real mean cuss. If both he and Slade are in town, you'd better hope they're on opposite sides.'

Charlie peered dubiously at the sergeant. 'D'you actually have any jurydiction in that town?'

Taylor was unable to stifle a chuckle. 'Don't you mean *jurisdiction*, you simple southerner?'

Rudabauer knew exactly what they both meant. 'This man Slade has murdered

154

seven US soldiers. That gives me all the authority I need. There's no law in that town, and if any of you have to kill someone, you do so under my orders. When we mosey on in there tomorrow, we'll have to play it by ear.' He glanced over at Bridger. 'If you spot anyone drawing a bead on us, trigger that big Sharps, you hear?'

The old scout favoured him with a toothy grin. 'It'll be my pleasure!'

*　*　*

The four horsemen made their way out of the rocks and took a circular route back on to the Bozeman Trail. That way, anyone watching their approach would think that the new arrivals had come from the south-east and there would be no inkling of Bridger's hidden presence. With the rising sun at their backs, the posse — because in reality that was what they were — advanced at a deliberate walk so as not to draw any special interest. Rudabauer's army uniform was unlikely to cause a stir. A deserter flocking to the latest gold strike was not a new phenomenon on the frontier.

Before they reached town, the sergeant had something to say. 'However this turns out, I want you to know that I'm grateful for your help,' he gruffly remarked. 'We were on opposite sides once, but thank God those days have passed. We've got new enemies to face together now.'

The former Confederates nodded their acknowledgement, but Waylan tempered their response. 'Just so there's no misunderstandings: *however* it turns out, when this is over, we're staying here to try our luck. There'll be no stockades, no trials and no army lynchings. Yeah?'

The grizzled non-com smiled. 'Yeah. Now get those Henrys on display. We don't want anyone thinking we're a soft touch.'

*   *   *

Jim Bridger placed the drawtube spyglass to one side and lifted the rear 'ladder' sight on his 'buffalo' gun. In his case that description was misplaced, because the buffalo was one of the few creatures that he hadn't actually made a habit of shooting. After setting the sights for two hundred yards, he then checked that the percussion cap was firmly seated on the raised nipple. On the rock before him were six paper cartridges and an equal number of caps. He well knew that if it did come to a fight, then it would be fast and furious . . . just like all those others over the past four decades and more.

Glancing over at the mining camp, he saw his four companions reach the first building. It had begun!

★   ★   ★

The Top Saloon was on the right-hand side of the thoroughfare and dwarfed its immediate neighbours. Henry Plummer appeared to be doing all right for himself.

Considering the hour, a surprising number of men were on the move, but then they were all headed the same way: out of town and away from the newcomers. Looking at the state of some of them, they were obviously returning to the diggings after a night of debauchery.

The arrival of four horsemen from the direction of the Bozeman attracted a deal of casual interest, but none of it hostile. Getting no response to their enquiries, the grubby prospectors merely shrugged and continued on their way. They had a day of unrelenting toil ahead, with the slim possibility of finding pay dirt.

Outside the saloon, a rough-and-ready hitching rail beckoned. Dismounting in front of it, the four men carefully scrutinized their surroundings, oblivious to the curious stares. Further down across the street was an imposing two-storey building with the legend 'Stuart's General Mercantile and Store' emblazoned across the front. Rudabauer raised his eyebrows. That was the other name that Wendell Storey had volunteered.

'Not *everyone's* in a hurry,' remarked Taylor softly.

Leaning against one side of the store was a snake-hipped gent, who seemed to be watching everything and nothing. He wore a tied-down gun and had very little dirt on his clothes. The sergeant nodded. The fact that his mouth was suddenly very dry had nothing to do with the warm weather. The harsh reality of what they were about had just hit home, because there could be little worse than tackling the unknown. Hoiking up some phlegm provided relief, as did the act of spitting it in the direction of the sinister bystander.

By pre-arrangement, Rudabauer and Waylan made straight for the saloon's double doors, leaving Taylor and Charlie to mind the horses and keep watch. The two point men glanced briefly at each other and exchanged grim smiles. Then they pushed on through the doors and entered Plummer's domain.

What they found offered little appeal. The large room stank from a toxic mixture of sweat, smoke and spilt alcohol. Tables and chairs were in total disarray and it was obvious that no one had yet begun to clear up after the long night. Only three persons were present, with just two being immediately noticeable. They were slumped face down over a beer-soaked table, snoring loudly. Saliva trickled from their open mouths.

'Oh, very nice,' Rudabauer muttered.

'This place looks like Sherman just marched right through it,' Waylan responded glumly. It hadn't escaped him that he and his friends intended remaining in Virginia City. If all the camp's saloons were like this, then there would be little to look forward to.

Then they noticed a lone individual sitting in the shadows at the rear of the room. On the table before him there was a coffee pot and a single mug. Off to his right at the back was an apparently closed door. With the flap on his military issue holster folded back behind it, the sergeant gestured to Waylan to move away slightly and then, in a loud voice, he addressed the solitary drinker.

'We're seeking the owner of this shi — establishment.'

'He ain't here,' came the unhelpful response.

'That's a shame. We've come an awful long way to give him some news.'

* * *

Slade's eyes snapped open. He knew instantly where he was and whom he held in his bear-like arms *and* why he was awake. The voice in the saloon was muffled, but still easily recognizable and last heard in Fort Phil Kearny. Retaining his hold on the nervous young prostitute, he whispered into her ear. 'You make a sound and I'll slit your pretty throat from ear to ear. Nod your head if you believe me.'

As expected, the abruptly terrified girl nodded swiftly and her 'lover' confidently released his grip. Swinging easily off Plummer's bed, he grabbed his revolver and padded over to the door. Although quite prepared to come out shooting, he was curious to find out how his new employer would react. On balance, he decided to wait on events.

*   *   *

'What kind of news?'

Rudabauer smiled knowingly. 'You'd need to be Mister Henry Plummer for me to tell you that.' He spotted a slight flutter of the other man's eyelids and knew that they'd got him.

Plummer stared hard at the weathered sergeant. He was puzzled. Most deserters tended to be disillusioned privates who quickly discarded their forage caps and other non-essentials, rather than seasoned non-coms in regulation uniform. And who was the hard-eyed youngster fingering the Henry rifle? 'Okay, so let's say that you've found him. Since when does the US Army deliver messages to saloon-keepers?'

'Since seven of its men were butchered!'

Plummer's poker-faced expression

162

momentarily slipped. 'What the hell's that got to do with me?'

'The man that did it works for you. Goes by the name of Slade. And you ain't just a saloon-keeper.'

Henry Plummer desperately tried to maintain control of his features, but behind the mask his mind was a seething cauldron. The fact that he didn't yet know the source of those last disclosures deeply troubled him. Could it be that somehow Wendell had turned against him? He also silently cursed his new employee's homicidal tendencies. Having unexpectedly discovered the gruesome scalps in Slade's saddle-bags, he did not doubt the sergeant's claim. Yet for the moment he couldn't afford to dwell on any of these matters. He had to decide on how best to respond. His eventual choice could have been more tactful.

'The God-damn army's got no jurisdiction in this city. So go kill a few savages. That's what you're paid to do, ain't it?'

Sergeant Rudabauer drew his service

revolver and surged across the room. Plummer's injured hand reached for his hideout gun, until he perceived the muzzle of the Henry pointing directly at his skull. Then all he could do was await the inevitable retribution that he had provoked. Rudabauer cocked his piece and painfully jabbed its muzzle into Plummer's forehead, bringing tears to that man's eyes.

'I'm under orders from Colonel Henry B. Carrington, Commander of the Mountain District, which covers all this territory and any other that he might lay claim to,' the soldier barked out, not entirely truthfully. 'My instructions are to capture this Slade and return him to Fort Phil Kearny for trial, and if you obstruct me you'll be going there too, tied over the back of a horse! So where is he?'

Frantically trying to marshal his thoughts, Plummer unwisely goaded his interrogator. 'This Carrington must be quite the peacock. What's the B stand for anyway?'

He was rewarded by the gun barrel

sharply rapping across the side of his head, as the sergeant rasped, 'Don't test me, mister.'

The saloon-keeper raised his hands imploringly. 'OK, OK, enough.' An idea had suddenly come to him that was exquisite in its simplicity. 'Slade is in town, but he don't work for me. The greedy bastard wanted more money than I could pay, so he went to work for the vigilantes. Which means you'd be doing me a real big favour if you carried him off, feet first or any which way.'

Rudabauer recoiled slightly. That was not an answer that he had been expecting. He glanced over at Waylan, but that man just shrugged and he suddenly wished that Jim Bridger were by his side. Then again, he didn't need the old scout to tell him that he hadn't had his question answered.

'You still ain't told me *where* he is.'

Plummer's eyes widened theatrically. 'Well hell, how should I know? I just done told you that he don't work for me.'

From off to the side, Waylan snapped

off a question. 'What's back of that door?'

The eyes remained wide, but the voice changed into a whine. 'It's just my bedroom, is all. Nothing of interest to you fellas in there.'

'We'll be the judge of that,' Rudabauer retorted. 'Anything happens to me when I open that door, blow his damned head off.' So saying, he strode over to the doorway and listened carefully.

Beads of sweat trickled down the saloon-keeper's face. Knowing Slade's predilection for violence, he genuinely thought that he was about to die. He instinctively flinched as the soldier stepped back and kicked out hard. The wood around the lock splintered and the door flew back on its hinges, allowing a certain amount of light into the room. What Rudabauer saw stopped him in his tracks.

A young woman, hardly more than a girl really, lay on the large bed. Totally naked and trembling with fear, she was apparently reluctantly awaiting Henry Plummer's return. Completely taken aback, the sergeant stared hungrily at her for a long moment, before finally managing to drag his eyes away and give the room a cursory examination.

'Cover yourself, girl,' he growled uncomfortably, suddenly recalling the revolver in his hand. 'You ain't got nothing to fear from me.' With that, he reluctantly reached out and pulled the door shut. As he returned to the saloon-keeper, his face wore a thoughtful expression. 'Seems like we might be keeping you from something.'

Plummer had a pretty fair idea what he meant. Winking slyly, he replied, 'Hee, hee. Well, a man's gotta live, eh?'

Rudabauer's features turned grim. 'So the sooner you help us, the sooner you get back to the poor bitch.'

Waylan had caught on, but stifled his interest and kept his rifle rock steady on target. At that moment, Hezekiah shuffled nervously into the saloon, with Charlie Pickett watching him closely from the threshold. The barman and various others were shortly due to start clearing up the night's mess. Although their timing was perfect for Plummer's nefarious purposes, he was concerned at the sight of another newcomer.

'Just how many of you fellas are there, anyway?'

'Enough,' was the curt response.

'Aw, shit,' exclaimed Plummer in a convincing show of resignation. 'Look gents, we're getting off on the wrong foot here. I've got a business to run . . . amongst other things. Why don't you take your horses down to the livery and get them took care of, and in the meantime I'll ask some questions of my own. Give me some time, yeah? Come back about noon. I should have some news for you by then.'

Rudabauer wasn't yet convinced. 'How do we know we can trust you?'

'You don't,' was the very plausible reply. After glancing over at Hezekiah, the saloon-keeper noticeably lowered his voice. 'Because let's face it, I ain't very trustworthy. But I do know a good deal when I see it. If you were to haul Slade out of here, then I'd have one thing less to worry about. Savvy?'

The sergeant glanced at Waylan, who nodded almost imperceptibly. 'OK, you got a deal. But if you double-cross us and I don't make it back to the fort, you'll have a whole lot more like me to cope with.'

'Sure, sure,' Plummer responded smoothly, before calling out to Hezekiah. 'Give these boys a keg of beer on the house. They must be mighty thirsty after such a long journey.'

'Obliged,' the soldier responded, finally holstering his sidearm. On the point of leaving, he glanced down. 'What happened to your hand?'

'Someone got careless!'

* * *

'Do you believe that son of a bitch?' Waylan asked, as the four men cautiously made their way towards the stables. Their short journey took them past Stuart's Mercantile, which was just opening for business.

'I think he'd sell his own mother to the Sioux,' Rudabauer growled. 'But I'll allow he does stand to gain from our arrangement.' He lowered his voice. 'If our fugitive *has* gone over to the other side. However you look at it though, it can't do any harm to rest up in the hay for a few hours and sup some of this Dutch milk.'

Waylan wasn't convinced. He'd seen the way that the sergeant had ogled the free keg of beer. Experienced veteran or not, some things about army life just never changed!

★   ★   ★

Hezekiah smelled a possible profit and consequently just couldn't help enquiring, 'You all right, boss? Those fellas looked kind of mean.'

Plummer nodded casually. 'They were just demonstrating their *bona fides* and sussing me out, is all. Men in their line of work can't be too careful, especially a deserter.'

Normally that would have been the end of the conversation, and so Hezekiah was mildly surprised when his employer sauntered over to join him near the bar.

'I reckon it'll soon be pay-back time for that cockchafer, Bunton, now that I've got some real hard cases on the payroll. Nobody carves *me* up and gets away with it.' He suddenly favoured his 'shit-faced' barman with a hard glance. 'That's just between you and me though, savvy?'

The other man feigned a look of pride, as though he welcomed such a display of confidence in him, which of course he did, but for other reasons. 'You can rely on me, boss.'

Plummer smiled and turned away, heading for his bedroom. Just before he reached the threshold, Hezekiah called out to him . . . as expected. 'Once the others get here, is it all right if I slip out for a while? I got a tooth that's giving me fits.'

'Yeah, sure,' replied the saloon-keeper smoothly. 'Can't have my top barman suffering.' With that, he tapped quietly on the damaged door and pushed it open. Even the sight of Slade suspiciously aiming a revolver directly at his chest couldn't dim Henry Plummer's glow of satisfaction.

10

Granville Stuart had a strong urge to crush the little toad under his boot, but as usual he managed to curtail the impulse. Hezekiah did occasionally come up with some useful information and this appeared to be one of those times. Consequently, Stuart was pressing the little turncoat hard and it didn't help the man's nerves that Bill Bunton was also looking menacingly on.

'So what you're saying is, Plummer's hired himself some new gun hands, yeah? The four men that turned up at his place earlier, yeah?'

Hezekiah nodded eagerly. 'That's right, Mister Stuart. He gave them a free keg of beer and they're in the livery getting their animals situated.' Glancing nervously at Bunton, he added, 'He intends settling scores with you for that knife wound.'

'The Beast' merely scoffed at that,

but Stuart hadn't finished yet. 'Free beer, huh? That's a first. Henry Plummer must really be getting desperate. My man held one of them to be a soldier.'

Hezekiah nodded eagerly. 'Plummer said he's a deserter. Now that the army's on the Bozeman, there's bound to be more of them coming up here.'

Bunton couldn't resist responding to that. 'That's what you reckon, is it? Well if that's true, how come we ain't seen so much as even one solitary son of a bitch arriving here on that trail in weeks?'

Stuart raised his hand. 'Except maybe the man that carved up young Jason. You seen any other strangers in town, Hezekiah?'

Without any hesitation, the barman shook his head. 'Nary a one, Mister Stuart.'

The other man stared at him long and hard, until finally he grunted. 'You've done well . . . this time. Do you want credit in my store or cash?'

Hezekiah didn't need to ponder that for long. Credit was only good if its grantor was still alive, and anyone could fall victim to a stray bullet. 'Cash please, Mister Stuart.'

*   *   *

With the snitch off his premises, Stuart lost no time. 'Seems like Plummer couldn't locate Slade and got a bunch of saddle-tramps instead. Pity. I just wanted to settle matters with him, not start a war.'

'So what do you want me to do?' Bunton enquired.

'I want a show of force. Round up all the men and go kill this deserter and his friends. And after that you'll have to show Henry Plummer just how Stuart's Stranglers got their nickname. He's led a charmed life for long enough and once he's out of the way I can really start to bleed this town.'

An unpleasant gleam had come into Bunton's eyes. 'If they're in the stables, how's about we burn them out? I'm partial to a good fire.'

Alarm flashed across Stuart's hard

features. 'Like hell you will! There's some of *my* horses in that livery, and besides you know what happened to my brother. Even his ma wouldn't have recognized him. Not that the old bitch could see worth a damn.' He thought for a moment before continuing. 'No, you wait them out and take 'em in the street. It'll make everyone realize that we're the new power in Virginia City.'

★ ★ ★

The girl had fled, sworn to secrecy and clearly terrified. Slade had made no secret of the fact that he wanted to send her straight down to the 'hot place', but Plummer didn't care to jeopardize his useful relationship with the whorehouse. And he had no doubt that she would keep quiet about Slade's presence, at least until the knowledge no longer mattered.

'You're my ace in the hole,' he remarked smugly. 'If that little shit Hezekiah sells his story properly, there's gonna be a bloodbath and whoever survives it will likely come looking for me. That's when you get to earn all that gold and show me just how good you really are. And then this town will finally be all mine to bleed dry!'

Slade grunted. With specie in his pocket and whores readily available, he had to admit that things were looking up. 'And what about this Hezekiah? You want him bled dry too?'

Plummer chuckled. 'Nah. Someone with half a brain comes in useful. I can work him like a puppet. I suggest you get to oiling them guns. I reckon you're going to need them soon.' He glanced over at the splintered wood around the lock. 'It's a pure shame about that door. I'd better get the undertaker to fix it, pronto. He's going to be way too busy afore long.'

* * *

Jim Bridger had viewed Virginia City's hustle and bustle with extreme distaste.

All his life he had attempted to keep clear of concentrations of humanity by travelling the high country, but he well knew that that aim was becoming increasingly difficult. And the coming of the railroads would irrevocably change everything. Most of the wild plains tribes hadn't yet recognized that threat, but the old mountain man knew better.

Through the spyglass, Bridger had watched as Rudabauer and Waylan entered the Top Saloon. He also spotted the apparently casual observer with the tied-down gun. A short while later, a runty looking individual followed them in, shadowed by Charlie. Not long after, the sergeant, carrying what looked like a keg of beer, came back into view with his young companion.

'God damn it all to hell,' Bridger had exclaimed. 'If he gets a skinful, he'll be of no use to man nor beast!'

He had then watched as the four men seemed to have a short discussion, before leading their horses over to the livery stables. Their short journey took them past a substantial two-storey building, which was soon to be the destination of 'runty'. Something about that man's furtive movements took his interest. He had stalked enough prey during his long life to realize that trouble was brewing.

Time passed, and a subtle but noticeable change came over the rough and ready thoroughfare: it had emptied of genuine prospectors, who had doubtless returned to the Alder Gulch diggings for the day, and was now occupied on the periphery by a band of far more threatening characters. Bridger counted fourteen of them. Some carried rifles and at least two had sawn-off shotguns. With all their attention focused on the livery, there could be no doubting their intentions, although the reason for them was not entirely clear.

The army scout sighed reflectively. This Slade was beginning to represent more trouble than he was worth, but there could be no turning back now. Taking up his 'truthful' Sharps, the hidden marksman sighted down its barrel. Whoever made the first move down there, he would be ready.

★   ★   ★

The three southerners silently regarded each other, frustration and annoyance visible on their features. Sergeant Rudabauer, who until very recently had given them no reason to doubt his competence, was greedily and noisily drinking from the upturned keg. It was as though the responsibility of his mission had suddenly overwhelmed him and Henry Plummer's free beer had given him an outlet. So much so that he hadn't even offered to share it.

The large livery building was further down the earthen street from Stuart's Mercantile, with rough shacks and grubby tents clustered on either side of it. Business was obviously good, because there were two stable hands on the premises, although strangely they had so far kept well clear of the newcomers, not even demanding money for feed and such.

Typically, it was Charlie who first voiced their fears.

'Something just ain't right about any of this. That poxy saloon-keeper could be up to anything while we're kicking our heels in here and that Yankee Sergeant's made himself a new friend, so he don't give a shit.'

Rudabauer belched noisily and settled down comfortably into the hay. Waylan glanced angrily at him. 'Well, that just tears it. Seems like we've hitched our wagon to an old soak, but I'm not for sitting around here. I vote we head on back to that saloon and see for ourselves what's happening. What say you?'

'Sounds good to me,' Taylor commented, levering up a cartridge out of the Henry's tubular magazine. It was the first time that the taciturn young man had spoken in ages, but his determination was plain to see.

'Right then,' Waylan returned. 'We hit that street like skirmishers, with space between us. Just in case.'

The three friends moved over to the

heavy double doors that fronted on to the street.

'Where y'all off to?' Rudabauer queried in surprise. 'Don't you even want a taste?' His words were slightly slurred, yet his wits hadn't completely left him, and as he began to comprehend the others' angry expressions, feelings of guilt assailed him. He was a career soldier, but nobody's hero. Indian fighting was a new and terrifying experience, and along with confronting Plummer in his saloon had obviously taken its toll.

'To do what you should be doing,' Charlie scathingly replied. 'Looking at you, it makes me wonder how the north won that damn war.'

The sergeant's eyes widened with both distress and anger, but he was given little time to respond. His reluctant companions were on the move. Taylor heaved open one of the doors just enough to allow Waylan room to slip through. The sight that confronted him filled him with dismay. The dusty thoroughfare was completely empty of prospectors, but they had been replaced by heavily armed men and one of them had a twelve-gauge pointed directly at him!

* * *

Jim Bridger grunted. There could be no doubt as to his first victim. As one of the stable doors opened, he took careful aim at a burly fellow brandishing a shotgun and squeezed the first of the double-set triggers. Even at over two hundred yards, he didn't for a moment doubt the outcome. Abruptly holding his breath, the sharpshooter squeezed the second trigger. With a comforting crash, the rifle fired, swiftly followed by a double discharge down on the street.

Without even bothering to view the result, he dropped the under lever to release the falling block breech and blew away the wisps of smoke. Swiftly taking up a paper cartridge, he slid it into the firing chamber and retracted the lever. Next, he flicked off the shattered remains of the percussion cap, replacing it with a new one. The whole process took mere seconds, so only when he had cocked the hammer did Bridger finally check the 'fall of shot'. What he saw made him smile with satisfaction.

★ ★ ★

Waylan desperately tried to swing his rifle muzzle over, but even as he did so he realized with dreadful certainty that he wouldn't make it. He was surely about to die!

As though by divine intervention, the gun thug with the sawn-off suddenly coughed blood and pitched forward, emptying both barrels harmlessly into the dirt as he did so. One of his comrades stared at him in horror and bellowed out, 'What the hell just happened?'

Bill Bunton, sensibly positioned to the rear of his men, heard the distinctive report from beyond the city limits and replied, 'Take cover! They're back of us as well.'

His men cottoned on fast and

scattered amongst the shacks on either side of the street, but not before another of them took a piece of lead in his left shoulder. With blood weeping from the mangled flesh, he reached cover of sorts and collapsed in the dirt.

Waylan seized the opportunity to race for the nearest tent, dropping to the ground behind it. The canvas wasn't proof against anything, but at least he was mostly hidden. Not quite sure what was going on, his two friends wisely stayed put. Sergeant Rudabauer, their supposed leader, peered suspiciously around, as though expecting to find more gunmen lurking in the livery. Only uncomprehending animals returned his gaze, because both stable hands had disappeared.

'Who the hell's doing the shooting?' he cried out petulantly.

'That tarnal saloon-keeper's done sold us out, you dumb son of a bitch,' Charlie angrily retorted. 'We're trapped in here like rats.'

The sergeant's expression changed to one of belligerence. Struggling to his feet, he shambled over to a pail of water and after removing his forage cap, abruptly thrust his head in it. Finally emerging, he violently shook himself, sending water everywhere as though he was some breed of shaggy dog. His eyes were red, but they held an alertness that had been missing for a while. Drawing his revolver, he joined the two young men by the entrance.

'So let's see what we're up against,' he barked. There was no mistaking the commanding tone that had returned. 'Get both doors open and then hunker down behind these bales of hay.'

His idea made sense, because as Charlie and Taylor complied, it became evident that the bales would still be in shadow. The three men would be able to view the street without being visible themselves. As expected, hasty shots rang out, but they remained untouched.

Deliberately and unhurriedly, the two southerners returned fire with their Henrys. Of Waylan there was no sign, but they were comforted by the sight of the cadaver in the street. It meant that Jim Bridger had his Sharps trained on their assailants, making up for the disparity in numbers. And then there followed a shouted exchange that was to alter everything.

Bill Bunton, frustrated by his unexpected casualties, hollered out, 'You, the deserter. Who the hell you got back of us?'

Rudabauer was both surprised and aggrieved. 'Who the hell you calling a deserter? I aim to be a sergeant major one day!'

Bunton shook his head in bewilderment, before yelling back, 'Well if you ain't a runaway, why in tarnation are you working for that ass wipe, Plummer?'

* * *

That particular 'ass wipe' was observing the whole encounter from the threshold of the Top Saloon, and realized that something had to be done, and fast. If the two sides began to parley, then his whole devious scheme would unravel.

Hezekiah watched with surprise as his boss raced to the back room, but that was nothing to the jaw-dropping shock that assailed him when he saw him re-emerge with a massively built bruiser carrying a Spencer Carbine. The two men moved on through the saloon, but stopped short of the entrance. It was here that Plummer explained the situation in detail and issued his instructions. 'If they all get to talking, my little scheme's gone the way of the beaver. Get up there in those rocks and make that sharpshooter bleed, while I stir them up again.'

Slade nodded confidently. 'He's a dead man.' With that, he slipped out of the door and into the alley to his left. He knew all about stalking human prey, and instinctively knew what was needed. Avoiding the main trail, he intended to make a wide detour and come up behind the hidden marksman.

On his way to the rear door, Plummer suddenly pulled up short in front of Hezekiah and unexpectedly drew his knife. Jabbing it towards the abruptly ashen-faced barman, he allowed it to draw blood on that man's chin and then snarled, 'You move from this spot while I'm gone and I'll slice you a new asshole. Savvy?'

Hezekiah, his eyes watering, made to protest, but what he heard next completely took the wind out of his sails.

'I know you've been feeding that cockchafer Stuart information. I've gone along with it because it suited me, but you're coming to the end of the line.'

The bartender could only nod dumbly. Fear and doubt overwhelmed him, and suddenly his Devil's pact with Stuart didn't seem so appealing.

Having made his point, Plummer hurried on into his room. Unbolting the rear door, he peered outside. The back alley was totally deserted. Gunfire had a way of doing that. Moving swiftly and taking advantage of his local knowledge, he paralleled the main street. In his un-injured left hand he clutched a cocked revolver, which was far from ideal, as he was right-handed. He had a shrewd idea where Waylan was likely to be, and so it proved. As he peered cautiously around the corner of a clapboard shack, he caught sight of the crouching young man. Without any hesitation the saloon-keeper fired.

* * *

Rudabauer glanced at his two companions. 'Something stinks here. Either that fella's lying and just trying to get us into the open, or that God-damn saloon-keeper has sold us down the river!'

'We done told you that already,' Charlie retorted with the hint of a smile.

At that moment a shot rang out off to their left, and Waylan howled with pain.

'The lousy bastards,' the sergeant exclaimed, his sojourn with the keg of beer now completely forgotten. 'Show them how you Johnny Rebs used to fight. No offence,' he hurriedly added.

'None taken,' Charlie replied as he opened fire.

Taylor had other things on his mind.

'Waylan,' he hollered. 'Are you hurt?' He breathed a sigh of relief as his friend immediately responded.

'Some cockchafer damn near took my ear off, but I'll live. They've got us pinned down good, though.'

'Maybe so,' Taylor countered. 'But while Bridger's back of them, they can't move either.'

The question was, how long would that man remain 'back of them?'

11

Jim Bridger smiled appreciatively as he gazed down on the mining town. Distance and high ground gave him an edge that was compounded by the presence of Rudabauer and the others. It meant that their opponents were unable to make a move in either direction without drawing fire. All he had to do was bleed them out one by one as they inevitably showed themselves. And at that very moment, the scout glimpsed a figure shifting position near the large mercantile building. 'Hmmm,' he intoned, and moved slightly to get a better shot.

The rock face in front of where he had just been exploded, unleashing jagged particles into the air. One of them struck him in the forehead, sending a wave of agony through his skull. Most men would have floundered around, leaving themselves open to the next shot, but the old mountain man was as tough as the land-scape. Knowing full well that he was under attack, he abandoned the waiting cartridges and rolled backwards. He had more in his pockets anyway and unless he could clear the blood from his eyes that fact would be irrelevant.

Slade snarled with anger and rapidly worked the lever action of his Spencer. Apparently, only lousy luck had caused him to miss his prey, but it meant that he would now have to work that bit harder. Retracting the hammer, he took swift aim at the moving target.

Bridger's diseased right hip jarred against a rock and he groaned. He was getting too old for all this shit. A second shot rang out and he heard something that sounded like a bee in flight pass by his right ear. Whoever was after him could sure as hell shoot!

Slade levered in another cartridge and then cautiously set off in pursuit. Who-ever was up there had dropped out of sight, which meant that he had irrevoca-bly lost the advantage of surprise. As his powerful legs carried him higher, he quelled the frustration boiling within him. Heightened emotion of any kind could easily get a man killed.

Moving by feel, the old man desperately retreated down the hillside. Still unable to see, he knew that he had to take a chance and stop for a moment. Crouching low, Bridger unfastened his neckerchief and moped his eyes and forehead with it. The material was soon soaked with blood, but at least his vision had returned. Quickly squeezing it out, he then tied it tightly around his head to staunch the flow. Next, taking up his Sharps, he again shifted position.

Slade guardedly reached his opponent's original firing position and immediately spotted the paper cartridges laid out in readiness. He smiled slightly. They told him that he was up against a single shot rifle. Accurate and powerful maybe, but a disadvantage in this kind of fight. Then he glimpsed the figure wearing some sort of weird headscarf and loosed off a shot.

Another bullet slammed into nearby rock, but this time Bridger caught a glimpse of movement back up near the summit. Instinctively, he fired and moved, but immediately regretted it. Yet another shot answered him, which meant that he was up against a repeating rifle and so couldn't afford to fire his own weapon merely for effect.

Slade had cursed and squeezed off another shot, before dropping down into a crouch. He'd felt the rush of air like a train pass him by. Whoever he was up against definitely had a big gun and knew his business. If he didn't want to end up felled like a buffalo, he would have to take great care.

* * *

Bill Bunton knew his weapons and discerned the different gunshots on the hillside. Then he spotted a large and vaguely familiar form moving up amongst the rocks. With other things on his mind, recognition eluded him, but he decided that somehow the situation had possibly changed for the better. And yet who was going to test that first?

An angry voice sounded off behind him. 'If you don't wrap this up soon, I'll start to think I hired me the wrong man!'

Bunton turned and found Granville Stuart's hard eyes boring into him. He choked off an obscene retort, and with great deliberation stepped out of the doorway. A bullet slammed into the timber near his head, but it was of a lower velocity and had come from the stables.

'Our back trail is covered, boys,' he bellowed to his men. 'We outnumber those sons of bitches three to one, so let's finish it now. Fifty dollars for the first man into that livery!'

Some of the wary gun thugs even managed a cheer, as a reinvigorated fusillade erupted from their firearms. A torrent of hot lead flew into the besieged building, tearing off splinters and kicking up dust. Sensing a turn of the tide, a number of the men began tentatively moving forward. It was payback time!

* ★ ★

Sergeant Rudabauer recognized the inevitable. 'We've opened up a real hornets' nest here. If those ass wipes decide to rush us or even set the place afire, we won't be able to hold them.'

'So what do you suggest, *sergeant*?' Taylor pointedly enquired.

'You boys came up here to do some prospecting, so let's find out just what the diggings are like. If we head off in the same direction that everyone else did, then we're sure to find them.'

The two southerners looked startled, but then Taylor caught on. 'You mean to make a fighting retreat — just like old Stonewall Jackson did so often with you Yankees. Spread 'em out and pick them off one at a time.'

Rudabauer nodded grimly, seemingly unconcerned by the slight. 'Uhuh. You up for it?'

'Damn right we are,' Charlie eagerly responded. Then, as the sergeant went in search of a rear door, he bellowed out through the main entrance. 'Waylan. We aim to do what ole Stonewall did to the Union so many times. You follow?'

A few seconds went by before they received a reassuring response. 'Sounds good to me.'

★ ★ ★

Over the constant gunfire, Bill Bunton heard snippets of the shouted exchange, but the veiled tactics meant nothing to him. He had sat out much of the long war, over the border, down Mexico way; looting, killing, despoiling senoritas and all the time *just* keeping one step ahead of the Rurales. Then return fire from the livery abruptly ceased and it occurred to him that maybe some of his men *might* be able to shoot worth a damn after all.

'We've done finished them, boys,' he yelled, stepping into plain sight and advancing rapidly on the stables. He didn't intend to waste any fifty dollars unnecessarily. Emboldened, his men followed and together they burst into the large building. They were greeted by a number of unsettled animals, but not a single human. Then one of his hired guns noticed an open rear door and raced over to it.

'Don't . . . ' Bunton hollered, but it was too late. A single shot rang out and the man fell back, spraying blood from a mortal wound to his throat. 'Forget the damn door,' he ordered. 'Spread out around the sides, and if you can't see anyone, at least aim at the smoke.'

Cautiously, his men did as ordered. Behind the stables were a few shacks and then broken ground leading off towards Alder Gulch. They caught sight of one of the fugitives as he disappeared behind a tree and then . . . nothing.

Bunton shook his head in dismay. 'God damn it all to hell,' he remarked to anyone listening. 'We should have torched the stables and to hell with the animals. Now we've got to hunt them down like dogs. Only the thing is, these dogs shoot back!'

It was a long time since Jim Bridger

had been under such pressure and he wasn't much enjoying it. His aching body was hot and sticky, and the gash on his forehead hurt like hell. Whoever he was up against knew both how to shoot and when to move. It occurred to him that his opponent could well be the murderous scoundrel they were seeking, but since he had never actually encountered him at the fort, that could only be conjecture.

Sounds of sustained gunfire drifted over the rocky hilltop, but he closed his mind to them. Then the front of a slouch hat appeared beyond a boulder and he knew that he was being tested with the oldest trick in the book. Holding his fire, Bridger decided to use the obvious ruse to his advantage and shift position. Keeping his finger clear of the hair trigger, he scurried to his right. His intention was to flank the other man, but the sudden explosion of pain in his left leg put paid to that.

Even as he fell sideways, the scout caught a glimpse of the muzzle flash above him and realized what had happened. The cunning devil had to have been stretched out full length, with his foot supporting the hat . . . and it had worked. If he hadn't been hurting so bad, he might even have heard the mocking laugh that accompanied his fall. Gritting yellowed teeth, Bridger dragged his tormented body out of sight. He wasn't sure whether his leg was broken or not and he didn't have time to try and staunch the flow of blood.

As he attempted to control the agony that had assailed him, he twisted around to survey his surroundings. The rocky hillside gave out shortly below him. After that, there was no cover worthy of the name. If he were to survive, he would have to turn the tables soon, before he bled to death!

Slade just couldn't resist a scornful laugh as he retrieved his hat and then shifted position. Whoever he was up against had just been taught a painful lesson by the master, and it was now time to finish the class. First though, he removed the tubular magazine from the butt of his Spencer and reloaded it. Only then did he demonstrate just what it was that made him so truly dangerous.

Sensing his opponent's weakness, the big man surged upright and began to leap apparently effortlessly from rock to rock. Superbly confident in his strength and speed, he allowed his massive leg muscles to carry him safely back and forth in a tremendous display of athleticism, all the time getting closer to his wounded prey. He had just landed on a smoothly rounded boulder when he glimpsed the Sharps muzzle emerging from between two rocks. Reacting instantaneously, Slade leapt sideways. He was entirely confident that the gun would be unable to traverse fast enough to get him.

With shocking force, the hunting knife buried itself in his left shoulder. The pain was so totally unexpected that even a man like Slade couldn't curb the scream that erupted from his mouth. He stumbled and only just stopped himself from crashing into a jagged rock. Even as he dropped down into a crouch, the hired killer realized that his own ruse had been returned in spades, and that he was apparently up against someone with similar skills. All of which meant that one of them was going to die very hard indeed!

⋆　⋆　⋆

The wet and grubby 'tin pans' working in and around the Ruby River looked up in surprise at the four men who approached them. One of them appeared to be an army sergeant, whilst another was bleeding from a cut to his ear. All of them were toting firearms, which unfortunately wasn't that rare in Alder Gulch, and immediately made the prospectors nervous. Some of them glanced at the old dugouts and wickiups that still remained from the early days, and contemplated withdrawing to them. It was the soldier who abruptly clarified the situation.

'We are being pursued by a gang of

assassins. Any of you men that don't want to die today would do well to hightail it out of here. I am under orders from Colonel Henry B. Carrington, Commander of the Mountain District, and we are *not* after your claims!'

Eyes wide with surprise, one of the prospectors gazed around at his fellows and remarked, 'You couldn't make up shit like that. I vote we leave 'em to it, at least for a while.'

The others stared intently at him for a moment before abruptly turning on their heels and fleeing into the trees on the far side of the shallow river. Casting them from his mind, Rudabauer carefully scrutinized his surroundings. It soon became apparent that he wasn't the only one doing that.

'Those old dugouts look kind of interesting,' Waylan opined as he unconsciously touched his bleeding ear. A number of them had been excavated near the river. Originally they had been covered with canvas, but were now open to the elements like military trenches. 'Two of us hidden in those and the others over in the trees might just answer.'

'It would be kind of like catching those sons of bitches between a rock and a hard place,' Charlie responded gleefully.

'I'd still like to know *why* all this is happening,' Taylor added thoughtfully. 'But maybe now ain't the time for that. They're coming!'

With that, the four men scattered, to await the next round of unnecessary bloodletting.

*   *   *

As usual, Bill Bunton advanced at the rear of his men and consequently remained unhurt when the ragged volley of shots tore into them. They had just reached the river's edge, and if Bunton's intelligence had matched his viciousness, he might have wondered just why all the prospectors had disappeared. As it was, two of his men crumpled to the dirt bleeding profusely and his numerical advantage dropped yet again.

'They're in the trees!' someone shouted.

'Like hell they are. They're using those dugouts,' responded another.

More shots rang out from both places and Bunton groaned. He was beginning to tire of this assignment. Now face down in the damp earth, he was conscious that his store-bought clothes were quite probably ruined, and he couldn't think of an easy way to finish what Granville Stuart had started.

★   ★   ★

Jim Bridger felt no satisfaction at having drawn the big man's blood. Apart from anything else, he was in too much pain from his damaged leg. Even if he survived this encounter, it appeared that he would have to tolerate two troublesome limbs from then on. Moaning with the effort, he reach out and grabbed the Sharps. Very conscious of where his opponent had landed, the battered scout then crawled awkwardly off in the opposite direction. Throughout every painful movement, he contemplated what to do next. He had to gain a decisive edge and the only way to do that was to delude the other man as to his whereabouts. But how to go about it?

Then, as he settled down behind yet another rock, an idea came to him. Not having adopted any form of metallic cartridge weapon, he still carried his black powder reserve in a flask attached to his belt. Laid on its side between some stones, with a fuse of loose powder ignited by a Lucifer, the result would be a sizeable detonation *and* a good distraction!

With his jaws clamped shut like a vice, Slade took a firm hold on the handle and extracted the blade in one swift move. His head swam and for a moment he almost lost his balance. Only an iron will had prevented him from crying out again. Angrily jabbing the knife into a patch of earth, he retrieved a grimy kerchief and stuffed it under his jacket over the throbbing wound. Then, gingerly, he attempted to move his left arm.

God damn, but it hurt! And it was obviously more than just a flesh wound, because there was no strength left and his hand would no longer form a fist. Although fuming with frustration, Slade nevertheless had sense enough to carefully survey his surroundings. His Spencer was cocked and ready, and there had never been a time when he couldn't use the weapon with only one good hand.

The ringing explosion took him completely by surprise. A few yards away, a dense cloud of smoke lifted into the air, whilst earth and grit landed all around. The big man was abruptly faced with a critical decision. How to react? Had the tricky bastard actually blown himself up by mistake, or was it just another ruse? Wait and see or make a move? Slade had always been inclined towards violent action, and so his instinctive response was to move. Drawing in a great breath, he leapt to his feet and launched himself forward.

Despite the waves of pain circulating around his body, Bridger couldn't restrain a grim smile as he rapidly drew a bead with his Sharps. He was a short distance behind the site of the detonation, so that momentarily he had his adversary full in his sights. As he squeezed the hair-trigger, his shoulder absorbed the satisfying recoil and he watched with relief as the massive fellow stopped in mid-stride.

Slade felt the hammer blow strike his chest and perversely the power suddenly drained out of his legs. Staggering to a halt, he gazed down stupidly at the blood on his jacket. 'How can this be?' he muttered as his right arm sagged under the weight of his Spencer. Then, a short distance ahead, he caught a glimpse of his nemesis. 'Sweet Jesus,' he cried. 'You're just an old man! I've been kilt by an old man!'

'Yeah, I'm old all right,' Bridger retorted. 'But *I'll* still see the next sunrise, which is more than you will.'

Slade slowly shook his head. 'Do you

even know who I am?'

The scout chuckled dryly. 'I'm guessing you go by the name of Slade. A low-down, murdering gun thug who'd kill his own mother for pay.' Even as he spoke, he began to reload the Sharps.

As Slade absorbed the insult, incandescent rage surged through him, temporarily negating the effects of the mortal wound. Nobody talked to him like that. He might be about to die, but he'd sure as hell take the old bastard with him. A great meaningless roar erupted from his mouth, as he both renewed his advance and took shaky aim with his rifle.

Jim Bridger couldn't believe his eyes as the massive brute again surged towards him. Desperately, he closed the breech, but instinctively knew that he didn't have time to level his own weapon — so instead he lurched to one side in an attempt to evade the wavering gun muzzle. By a second trick of fate that day, his wounded leg gave way just as the other man fired. The bullet tore across the back of his coat, tearing the material and painfully scoring his flesh . . . but he survived.

With a howl of frustration, Slade dropped the Spencer and drew his knife. Blood loss was making him light-headed, and it was pure hatred and strength of will that kept him on his feet . . . just. With a last great effort, he lunged towards the fallen scout.

Just at the last moment, Bridger heaved his Sharps upright and cocked the hammer. Slade was so close that his muscular belly suddenly thrust against the gaping muzzle and it was then that his opponent squeezed both triggers. The gun went off with a great roar and literally blew a hole through Slade's stomach. No mere mortal could absorb such treatment, and this time his legs finally failed him. With his whole torso literally drenched in blood, the massive killer fell to earth. As the light finally began to drain from his eyes, Slade suddenly had a flash of intuition.

'You're that . . . old bastard, Bridger. Ain't you?'

'Jim Bridger, *mountain* man,' that individual responded with something like pride.

'I . . . hope . . . that . . . leg . . . infects!'

'Maybe, maybe not. But you won't live to see it!'

12

Henry Plummer's jaw literally dropped in horrified amazement at the sight before him. His much feared and seemingly indestructible hired gun was being dragged feet first down the main street, behind a horse ridden by a bloodstained old man. The same rope that ended up wrapped around his killer's saddle horn had tightly bound Slade's ankles. And there could be no doubt at all that the huge assassin was actually dead, because the saloon-keeper had never before seen so much fresh blood coating one man. It was as though he had been hauled through a slaughter yard on the way into town.

Plummer felt the old man's hard eyes flit over his and hastily stepped back into his premises. His heart was thumping like an anvil strike. Just what the hell was he to do now? Completely oblivious to the few hard-drinking customers that were dotted about his premises, he fled to the sanctuary of the back room and desperately tried to come to terms with what he'd just witnessed.

Distant gunfire was still audible, and yet the new arrival had been heading directly for it, which meant that he was obviously seeking to rejoin his four companions. With Slade dead, the army no longer had any business in Virginia City, but as before, if they should get to talking with Bill Bunton, then Henry Plummer's future would be very bleak indeed. The problem was, how to prevent that from happening? Then a doozy of an idea suddenly leapt into his febrile mind.

Forget the morons on wages, fighting it out near the diggings. If he took advantage of Granville Stuart's temporary isolation and killed him, he could then hightail it out of town for a few days to let the dust settle. Without a paymaster, Stuart's men would soon drift away and of course the army would go back to fighting Indians like they were supposed to, instead of hassling honest businessmen like him. As he began to smile at the prospect, an even more agreeable idea came to him. In a form of poetic justice, he would use Hezekiah to assist him with the killing.

★   ★   ★

Jim Bridger knew that his wounded leg needed attending to, but it would have to wait until his companions were out of danger. Finding them was easy. Unlike the others, he had scouted the area in times past. The sound of shooting grew louder as he passed through the town and then on towards the Ruby River. Occasionally the trailing corpse snagged on some obstacle, but he urged his horse forward regardless. To his mind, it was just a shame that Slade wasn't still alive to enjoy it!

Coming to the crest of a rise, he saw the river open out before him. Proof of the gold prospectors' activity was everywhere to see, but his only interest was in preventing any more killing. A number of men were lying about near the bank of the shallow river, unleashing the occasional shot into the trees or at the dugouts. That had to be where Rudabauer and the southerners were hiding. Sighing, Bridger wheeled his horse around and awkwardly dismounted. He limped painfully over to Slade's body, which at least confirmed that his leg wasn't broken. He grabbed the rope and lifted the legs as high as possible.

'You fellas, down there,' he hollered. 'There ain't no need for any of this. We've got what we came for.'

A reaction shot rang out that kicked dirt up nearby, but Bridger kept his nerve and didn't retaliate. Instead he tried again. 'This cadaver, name of Slade, is all we sought. He's wanted by the US Army.'

Now that did get a response. Bill Bunton bellowed at his men to cease firing, before twisting around to scrutinize the stranger on the hillside. 'That son of a bitch always was right popular,' he drily remarked. 'And you're saying that really is Slade you got up there? Dead . . . stone cold dead?'

'Uhuh.'

'And you kilt him all on your lonesome?'

'It sure weren't easy, but yes, I did.'

Bunton shook his head in amazement. 'Just who the hell are you, mister?'

'His name's Jim Bridger,' Rudabauer bellowed out from the tree-line. 'He used to be a mountain man and now he scouts for the army. Right now he works for me.'

Bunton gently lowered the hammer on his revolver. He'd got the way out that he wanted, but one thing still rankled. 'You know how many dead we got?'

'You started it,' retorted the sergeant. 'And just be glad you didn't kill us, because then you'd have had the 18th Infantry on your back.'

There really wasn't anything he could say to that, so Bunton gratefully clambered to his feet, holstered his side arm and once more peered up at the bloodied scout. Shaking his head again, he remarked, 'Everybody's heard of you, but I thought you'd been paroled to Jesus years ago!'

Bridger was beginning to feel faint, but still managed to summon a response. 'Not hardly, but I'll allow that this big cuss nearly got the job done.'

★   ★   ★

Hezekiah could feel his guts churning at the prospect of acting as point man to a killing. *But* he could also see the potential of *permanently* acting as a turncoat. He had always fancied running his own saloon and taking his pick of the available whores. The trick, as always, was to try and stay alive long enough to realize it. It had never occurred to his unimaginative mind that there might be more to running a business in a town without any law than just fornicating with the employees!

'Remember,' snarled Plummer, as they crossed the street. 'That bastard doesn't know that I know about your little arrangement. So let's keep it that way 'til I get him under my gun. If this turns out OK, you might just get to keep your job *and* your life.'

Very conscious that Plummer was close behind him with a revolver in his left hand, the duplicitous bartender gingerly opened the door into Stuart's Mercantile. As expected, the store was deserted. A serious shootout usually achieved that. As his boss followed him in, Hezekiah pointed to the flight of stairs behind the well stocked counter and received a curt nod. The scrawny little fellow was filled with trepidation as he began to mount the steps. His state of mind wasn't improved when Stuart's voice boomed out from above.

'You'd better have something good for me, Bunton!'

Hezekiah swallowed hard before replying. 'It ain't him, Mister Stuart. It's me, Hezekiah. You know, the barman from the Top Saloon.' That last bit was purely gratuitous, because he had no doubt that Stuart knew exactly who he was. He just prayed that Plummer didn't spot it.

'What the hell do you want?' came the discouraging response.

'Plummer's had news about that real mean cuss, Slade. I thought maybe you'd like to hear it.'

There was a moment's silence before a reply was forthcoming. 'Well then, I guess you'd better come on up.'

The two intruders heard footfalls on the wooden floor above and then all was silent. They glanced at each other, before Plummer impatiently gestured that his employee should continue climbing. Hezekiah very reluctantly complied, and soon found himself emerging into a poorly lit office of some kind. Directly before him was a desk. It was only when he reached the top of the stairs that he realized there was a figure behind it.

Then a gun muzzle appeared and the barman thought his time had come, but it suddenly jerked sideways twice. The instruction was obvious, and Hezekiah rapidly followed it. As he stepped away from the top of the stairwell, Henry Plummer's head emerged and a single shot exploded in the enclosed space. The doomed saloon-keeper never even got the chance to register his horror. A large calibre bullet ploughed through his skull and sent him tumbling back down the stairs in a flurry of blood and dust.

With eyes as wide as saucers, Hezekiah timidly peered down at his former employer. His broken body lay in a spreading pool of blood and brain matter. There could be little doubt as to his condition.

'I presume he's dead,' came the matter-of-fact enquiry.

'Oh, he's dead all right, Mister Stuart. Very dead. Dead as a wagon tyre, in fact. Hee hee.' As a cloud of acrid powder smoke seemed to envelope him, the new proprietor of the Top Saloon felt strangely lightheaded and not a little giddy. It didn't help that his ears were ringing painfully from the awful detonation.

'That's that, then,' Granville Stuart remarked, as he casually rose from his swivel chair, revolver still cocked and ready. 'I suppose I'd better see what's occurring outside.'

'How's about I tag along, Mister Stuart?' Hezekiah queried hopefully. 'I need to talk to you about the saloon. It's owner having just died, an' all.'

Stuart favoured him with a questioning glance, which abruptly changed into a thoroughly unpleasant grin. 'No, you stay here,' he remarked, as his finger squeezed the trigger.

Shocking agony erupted in the new saloon-keeper's belly, and as he foolishly looked down, he suddenly realized that his cotton shirt seemed to be on fire. Stuart briefly regarded the smouldering weasel with disdain, before smashing his gun barrel against the side of his victim's head and then giving him a good hard shove. The stricken fellow toppled head first back down the stairs and landed directly, belly to belly, on top of his former boss.

'That's one way to put out a fire,' Stuart remarked, vaguely annoyed that there was no one to appreciate his sparkling wit.

Fastidiously avoiding the disgusting mess at the bottom of the stairs, he cautiously left the building. It occurred to him that he wouldn't like to be the man that had to clear up that lot.

* * *

'You're not figuring on hauling this big oaf back to the fort, are you?' Bridger enquired wearily. 'Because in this heat he'll turn for sure.'

Rudabauer regarded the battered old frontiersman with great warmth. All the good things that he'd heard about him had turned out to be true. Nevertheless, there was sound reasoning behind what he was about to propose . . . at least by his reckoning.

'We're gonna wrap him in a tarpaulin and take him back to Fort CF Smith. It's on our way and I reckon that captain will look real favourable on me . . . us . . . for producing the cuss that slaughtered all his men. Don't you think? *And*, if he does start to ripen, the smell will, like as not, cover the stink of greenrod if it takes a hold in your leg.'

Despite his body's various sources of pain, Bridger just couldn't restrain a great belly laugh at that. 'You're a real peach, ain't ya?'

The three southerners, who had finally accepted that a ceasefire existed, joined in the laughter, although theirs was far more restrained. Having quite possibly made a lot of enemies in Virginia City, they were all troubled about their own future. It was then that their attention was taken by the approach of a big, hard-looking individual on horseback. He made straight for the man known as Bunton, and a long, and at times heated, discussion ensued.

'No need to guess who they're jawing about,' Waylan remarked. 'I'll wager it's his men we've been shooting at.'

At length, Bunton strode over to introduce his boss. 'This here's Mister Stuart. He kind of . . . runs things in this town.'

That man carefully scrutinized the

five newcomers before speaking. His glance noticeably lingered on Bridger's craggy features. 'As Bill said, I run things here. Especially since Henry Plummer just checked out . . . permanently.'

Rudabauer grunted. 'This ain't a town. It's just a shit hole ruled by greed, but I'm kind of glad to hear about Plummer. He had it coming for starting all this gunplay.'

Stuart regarded him shrewdly. 'So we'll all let bygones be bygones, huh? I got no fight with the army. Hell, you might bring me some business one day.' He turned to Bridger and held out his hand. 'And I've heard all about you. You've done me a real big good turn, putting Slade out of my misery. He had a big hand in killing my brother. If you ever need to call the favour in, you know where to find me.'

The old scout took the proffered paw and offering a wry smile, held on to it. 'I don't reckon I'll be back this way again, so I'm going to take you up on that right now.'

Stuart raised his eyebrows, but offered no other response.

'Working under my orders, these three young fellas could well have killed some of your men, but they want to stay around and do some prospecting. I want your word that no harm will come to them, now or anytime in the future. If it does, I'll be back. And I live by the feud!'

The two men stared into each other's eyes for seemingly an age, before Stuart finally nodded. 'You have my word. There is one other thing you could do for me.'

Bridger waited expectantly.

'Allow me to take one of Slade's ears. Pickled in a jar, it'll remind me that I finally avenged my brother.'

Jim Bridger laughed. The prospect didn't bother him at all. He'd cut bigger parts off bigger creatures in his long life. Unsheathing his own knife, he replied, 'Might as well use mine. That bull turd has already had a taste of it.'

13

The three southerners gazed with genuine affection at the two mounted men. Any sour thoughts carried over from the long war had completely dissipated. And although the momentous events of the previous day were still raw and fresh in their minds, they at least now appeared to have a future ahead of them. Sergeant Rudabauer had assured them that his report to the colonel would confirm that, following Slade's death, they had fled the territory. Backed up by Bridger's testimony, such an account would be accepted as gospel.

The old mountain man had had his leg bound up and insisted that he was ready to travel. In truth, he detested his urban surroundings and intended to rest up at Fort CF Smith. He owed it to himself to relax in the sutler's store for a while. And with Slade's corpse strapped securely over the back of a trailing horse, they were guaranteed a warm welcome from the post commander. So, with nothing else to detain them in Virginia City, it was definitely time to leave.

Rudabauer reached down to shake hands with the three men. 'You fellas keep out of trouble, now. You hear?'

Charlie and Taylor grinned and winked at him, whereas Waylan appeared uncharacteristically pensive. He gestured towards the cadaver. 'I know he carried out lots of bad deeds, but that man did save my life.'

Jim Bridger snorted dismissively. 'Maybe so, but back down the trail a-ways you said he had a motive for that. Like as not, he wanted to turn you into a hired gun. Don't you go forgetting that.'

Waylan smiled and nodded. 'Yeah, I guess so. Anyhu, it's been a real pleasure knowing you, Mister Bridger. Don't go and get yourself ambushed on the way back. That'd be just a crying shame.'

It was Sergeant Rudabauer who had the last word. 'Don't you worry about us, Waylan Summers. There ain't a man born that can kill this old mountain man, and that's the God's honest truth!'

*   *   *

Wendell Storey sighed with relief. It really appeared as though he had made good his escape. His hands were badly blistered from cutting hay, and he now harboured a real dislike of the US Army, but at least he'd finally got clear of the God-damned bluecoats. Having stoved one young soldier's head in, Storey had taken his Springfield and a horse and ridden like the hounds of hell were after him. Only after having covered a good few miles had he eased off to take stock.

Thankfully, he had fled in the right direction: north-west and back on the Bozeman Trail towards the relative tranquillity of Virginia City. God help him if he hadn't actually missed that tricky bastard, Henry Plummer. His biggest regret, apart from the knife wounds inflicted by that maniac Bridger, was the loss of his

Colt Dragoon. The old horse pistol had been with him for years and a muzzle-loading rifle was no fair substitute.

As his breathing gradually returned to normal, the bovine thug scrutinized the apparently deserted terrain. He was surrounded by lush grass and groves of pine trees. With the sun warming his body, a more imaginative man might have appreciated the beauty of his surroundings. As it was, the unspoilt land was just an obstacle to cross.

From off in the trees to his right came the strangely insistent sound of bird song. It wasn't anything that he could put a name to, and yet surprisingly it was immediately answered with even greater clarity from a stand of trees on his left. For a moment he was perturbed, but then he shook his head and laughed out loud. After all he'd gone through, the last thing he needed to worry about was a flock of poxy birds!

We do hope that you have enjoyed reading this large print book.

Did you know that all of our titles are available for purchase?

We publish a wide range of high quality large print books including:
Romances, Mysteries, Classics
General Fiction
Non Fiction and Westerns

Special interest titles available in large print are:
The Little Oxford Dictionary
Music Book, Song Book
Hymn Book, Service Book

Also available from us courtesy of Oxford University Press:
Young Readers' Dictionary
(large print edition)
Young Readers' Thesaurus
(large print edition)

For further information or a free brochure, please contact us at:
Ulverscroft Large Print Books Ltd.,
The Green, Bradgate Road, Anstey,
Leicester, LE7 7FU, England.
Tel: (00 44) **0116 236 4325**
Fax: (00 44) **0116 234 0205**

Other titles in the
Linford Western Library:

VALERON'S JUSTICE

Terrell L. Bowers

Brother and sister Nash and Wendy Valeron didn't expect that starting up a doctor's practice would be so lively. But when a young woman rushes in and begs them to hide her, their lives are turned upside down. What begins as protecting Trina from a couple of bullies turns out to include land grabbing, murder, and a corrupt asylum. Only the combined strength and savvy of the Valeron family can foil the wrong-doers' sinister plans. Who will be left standing after the blood and gunsmoke finally clear?